A Horse Called El Dorado

KEVIN KIELY was born in Ireland and began writing in his teens. As well as two collections of poetry, he has published novels for adults, had plays broadcast on RTÉ and engaged in literary journalism and editing.

He has a wide range of work experience, including teaching, lecturing, horticulture, quality control, caretaking, deliveries and house painting. He has received five Literature Bursary Awards from the Irish Arts Council, and is Honorary Fellow in Writing with the University of Iowa. He has lived in Europe and the US but is settled in Ireland.

Acknowledgements:

Much thanks and gratitude for taking in this story to Michael O'Brien and Íde Ní Laoghaire. Thanks also to Kunak McGann, Emma Byrne, Eoin O'Brien for editorial guidance, Maeve McCarthy for artwork, Eanna Kiely for the initial impetus and Shane Kiely for solid advice.

A Horse called
EL DORADO

Kevin Kiely

THE O'BRIEN PRESS
DUBLIN

First published 2005 by The O'Brien Press Ltd,
20 Victoria Road, Dublin 6, Ireland.
Tel: +353 1 4923333; Fax: +353 1 4922777
E-mail: books@obrien.ie
Website: www.obrien.ie

ISBN: 0-86278-907-9

British Library Cataloguing-in-Publication Data
A catalogue reference for this title is available from the British Library.

1 2 3 4 5 6
05 06 07 08 09 10

The O'Brien Press
receives assistance from

Editing, typesetting, layout and design: The O'Brien Press Ltd
Cover illustration: Maeve McCarthy
Printing: Cox & Wyman Ltd

Dedication:

For my wonderful children Laura and Ruadhán,
who say I can't stop telling stories.

Chapter 1

I was born in Colombia, a country as large as France, Spain and Portugal put together. Maria Torres, my mama, is from one of Colombia's big cities, named Cali. My wandering Irish papa, Joseph Carroll, is from Fordstown, County Meath. He looks like Grandad, and people say that I have a look of them both. I arrived in Ireland for the first time when I was thirteen.

Mama, Papa and I lived far from any city in a *comuna*, or commune, on the banks of the Río Putumayo, a river that goes on for hundreds of miles and flows into the Amazon. When I close my eyes I sometimes feel that I can still smell the air and the flowers. Colombia has the most beautiful flowers in the world. There are orchids of every colour, clumps of them going on and on, bright enough to make your eyes blink in wonder. There are trees with sword-shaped leaves, and enormous ferns, higher than any building in Ireland. There is heat all day during the long summers. Colombia is near the Equator, the hottest part of the world.

The commune was in the region of the Caquetá and Putumayo, in the south of the country. We lived off the land, growing our own food, which meant a lot of hard work, digging and planting. I had my own bow and arrows in case some jaguar or ocelot, big jungle cats, came prowling out of the heat and mist. It is not all jungle and forests in that region – there is much tree felling and burning of land to make space for growing crops.

I loved the jungle, but I was a little afraid of it and I would never wander in too far. Where I lived there were monkeys, and sometimes they would howl and call to each other all night. The birds would put me into a trance when I was young as I stopped to hear the sounds they made from their multicoloured beaks. I'd stare up at the hummingbirds until my neck hurt. Enormous toucans flew out of the forest and always put me in a crazy mood with their hooting and shrieking. Their rapid flapping from branch to branch on the trees would make me want to run wild.

The commune was a sprawling little village made up of huts of different sizes, all with roofs made of down-sloping layers of leaves. When it rained the water would roll from one layer to the next and down onto the mud. There was a tool hut and a big food storage hut as well as a meditation hut, also used for meetings and business, with a wooden sign on the roof which said, 'Make it Eden'. The sign was made by a big American man called Hank Shepak, a drifter from Colorado who always laughed at his own jokes. No-one else did, but everyone agreed that he was a good organiser.

The huts were linked by walkways of planks placed on

the mud. There was a television, a video player and a computer, locked in storage cupboards in the meditation hut. Our electricity came from a generator that often broke down. The commune also owned a small truck, so that we could travel to El Encanto, a little town along the river. We were 'friends of the Earth', and the adults wanted the whole world to become a commune some day. We mostly spoke Spanish at the commune, but various other languages were spoken too. I learned English from my papa and from Paul Rooke, and I also know a few words of German, Dutch and Portuguese.

There were other kids at the commune, and not all Colombian. Erica Van Egden from Holland had a daughter called Carlotta, who was older than me, and Greta Meissner, from Germany, had two young sons. Some of the men were good to us but others did not want kids around too much, so we kept out of their way. Paul Rooke, another American, always wore a leather headband and he played a saxophone at our *fiestas*, or parties. He was good to me because I shared his love of horses, but Mama didn't trust him. I hung out with Paul Rooke and a local man named Gonzales, but mainly I liked to spend time with my friends César, Jésus, Martha and little Jaime.

When I was very young, I'd sometimes see the huge wings of gliding condors and think they were small aeroplanes in the distance. Then I would run to Mama. She would hug me and take me out of the sun into the

9

hut and we would play with the mirror and her combs. My hair is brown but hers is black, thick and shiny. Mama used to tell me a story about the Putumayo river. It stopped flowing every night, she would tell me, and every morning as soon as the sun rose over the Andes it would wake, start to bubble, splash and suddenly get up and roar along again.

Around the time I was seven or eight, Mama went with a new man. I told everyone in the village because I felt scared and angry, and maybe that was the cause of the boxing match, between the men who fought over her. One of the men was my papa, Joseph. Well, he left a few days after that fight, bruised and with a cut on one cheek. He explained to me that Mama was going to live with the other man and that I would be okay. Then my papa went one morning with his haversack and his guitar, a *cuatro*. I watched him walking down to where the riverbank path goes beyond many mud paths and far off towards the Andes mountains. I had tears in my eyes. I couldn't see if he had any tears, but he raised a fist and shook it at the Heavens. He turned back a few times after that, and finally disappeared.

The Andes mountain range looked threatening in the distance, like a massive dark cloud on the horizon that never moves. For months after my papa left I used to think that he was in some village in the Andes. I heard stories from passing wanderers about those places, where it gets so cold at night that they have to sleep beside fires and wrap up in many blankets. The Andes seemed so far away that I hardly thought they were real, but one day I would cross those mountains. Papa occasionally sent an e-mail to the commune. Mama would bring me the page and read his words so I knew he was still somewhere and asking about me.

Mama did not live too long with her new man. I slept in one of the communal huts with the boys and girls, while she moved in with the other women. Mama kept away from men after that, except when she was working with them in the fields.

Paul Rooke and Gonzales looked after the horses in the corral, a fenced-off area in the shade of high trees. Here I learned to ride and Paul said I was 'a natural'. I really liked one of the horses particularly, a beautiful horse called El Dorado. He was a gorgeous golden colour, and when he galloped along the riverbank he seemed to glisten in the sunlight. I grew to love him and soon understood that he would not obey anyone except me and Paul Rooke. If others went near him he would shy away. When the adults got rough with him he would move back and prepare to defend himself. By the time I was eight everyone in the commune said that Pepe and El Dorado were inseparable. I liked that.

The horse was named after the legend of El Dorado, which Gonzales had told me. It was about an ancient king who covered himself in gold dust and went out on a raft into the middle of a big lake, *Laguna de Guatavita*.

He flung in gold bars and jewels as an offering to the gods for his wife, who had drowned herself because she was unfaithful to him. Then the king jumped in to wash off the gold dust. Long before that, the Muisca Indians of the area also emptied gold, emeralds and food into the lake as tributes to the gods.

Chapter 2

My life was very primitive in the commune. At least, Grandad and Grandma tell me so, having heard my story. At the commune we had no use for money. We exchanged what we grew – coffee, sugar, maize, potatoes, bananas, kidney beans and cocoa – for other items we needed, such as diesel for the truck and the generator. Fruit was all around at harvest time – not in boxes and stands like in a supermarket with labels and prices, but growing on the trees and bushes around us. We stored bunches of bananas and pineapples in baskets made out of leaves.

We would never waste food, because it is a gift from the planet. If a crop gave us a rich harvest we would have a party. The adults made beer out of maize. Sometimes it was good and they cheered, drinking it down, shouting 'chicha' to each other and laughing.

The sprawling village commune had a good view down onto a narrow stretch of the Putumayo river. Across the river the jungle was thick and dark. I would look across at it and think I saw strange sights among the shadows – giant beings, flying saucers and ghosts.

Small tribes of jungle indians would sometimes appear

under the tall trees. We knew not to stare at them or move close to them, because they feared us. I was quite afraid of them too when I was small, but Mama always said that they were peaceful. The adults knew the tribes by name – the Andokes and the Huitotos, who had been cannibals according to legend and long ago worked for the whites collecting rubber from the *hevea* trees. These tribes hunted using short spears and the *sumpitan*, or blowpipe, that shot poison darts. They wore little cloth-ing, but a lot of face paint and feathers in their hair. They looked very ancient, as though they were made of stone.

One year everyone at the commune worked hard to make a rope bridge for crossing the river. First, the adults had to saw logs for the bridge and to build scaffolds on each side of the river. Then they made a raft for going over to the other side. It seemed like magic, the way everybody, working together, got the bridge to span the river in one long, hot day. Our group were not stupid donkeys, as Mama would say. We shouted and cheered when the first couple walked over and back. A large hut was built on the other side of the river, hidden carefully among the trees, 'In case of trouble,' as Paul Rooke said.

Even with all the hard work, living in the commune was like paradise to us. Well, almost. There was some bad stuff too. You must have heard about drugs on televi-sion? It's serious stuff, and guys get put in prison for a long time for selling them. Well, Colombia is one place where a lot of drugs are grown and harvested, mostly cocaine and cannabis. Cocaine is made from *coca* leaves, which are green and oval in shape. If you chew the leaves they give you energy. The Indian tribes use them as a tropical medicine.

Then there is AGRA, which stands for *la Agrupación Radical Anticapitalista* – a big, long name for a bunch of thugs who drive around in jeeps with rifles and machine guns. I saw them several times and still have bad dreams about them sometimes. Have you ever heard a gunshot? It is like a loud, cracking noise and it shocks, deafens and scares you. If you saw the things that I've seen, you'd have bad dreams too.

Those heavies with the guns I mentioned, the dirty AGRA, are in the drug business. They are what we call *narcotraficantes* – a much feared word, and not because it is so big. It means they are drug dealers, people who kidnap, who take hostages, who steal and who kill. Some people say AGRA help the poor, but everyone in the commune feared them. Sometimes government soldiers passed near to the commune in trucks looking for them. But mostly the government were afraid of AGRA too.

AGRA ended my time in the commune. That was the biggest adventure of my life. But my newest adventure will be even greater. I just know it will.

Chapter 3

Did you know that trouble can come as quick as lightning? It cracks off like gunshots. And one night trouble came to the commune. I remember Mama shaking me. She had come into the communal hut where I slept with the other children. One of her hands covered my mouth and there was fire in her eyes. In the lantern light they looked like shining jewels.

'Pepe,' she whispered, 'go to your tree house and be careful you are not seen. Do not leave, no matter what you hear.' I knew from the sound of her voice that every word she said must be obeyed. Mama was shaking. I felt like gasping for air and rubbing my stomach to make it stop heaving.

The moon was at the top of the sky and it lit the path to my hideout, a long run away from the huts. I climbed up to the tree house and pulled the rope ladder up after me. I was safe then, looking down over the commune and the river. The bright moonlight clearly showed our little village, with all its familiar huts. I could see the adults busily running about, moving things. The television, the computer, boxes of food and other valuables were loaded into the truck. Gonzales got in and drove slowly, without headlights, until he stopped some distance away and switched the engine off. Others were slashing branches from trees with their machetes and collecting the leaves to camouflage the truck. The horses were led quietly in amongst the trees and tethered in a hidden place.

Then the women and the other children all hurried over the bridge to the secret hut on the other side of the river. All the commotion ended quite suddenly, and the commune grew very quiet.

The moon had seen it all and her face stared down blankly. At least she could tell no-one our secret. I curled up in my hideout, yawning and gripping my knees. Everywhere there was silence, except for the sound of the river. Even the jungle was quiet that night. My gut instinct told me that something would happen.

I do not know which I noticed first, the noise of the jeeps or the headlights. The engines were revving as they bumped their way up the mud path along the river bank. My eyes and mouth were wide open and I sat like a statue as the headlights showed up parts of the trees and then the huts. Loud music blared from the sound system in one of the jeeps, music with drums, bells, trumpets and guitars. The music was so loud, I felt as if my ears would burst. I was dizzy with fear. It was the guerrillas, the dreaded AGRA. I was glad now that Mama and all the other women and children were in hiding across the river, but the men were still in the huts, taking their chances.

The jeeps stopped in the middle of the commune, honking their horns, their headlights shining starkly on our huts. I was frightened of what would happen, but I could not look away. Soon the men of the commune were rounded up at gunpoint and counted. They huddled together in a line, shivering, their faces down on their chests. The guerrillas marched around them shouting abuse and questions. It felt strange to be sitting there in my tree house, watching everything that was happening, but invisible to everybody below. I was as safe as a bird in my tree, except I could not fly away.

'No tenemos nada aqui,' Gonzales muttered to one of them that had poked him in the stomach with a weapon. That's Spanish for, 'We have nothing here.' The AGRA guerrillas searched the huts, dragging Paul Rooke with them as their prisoner and beating him occasionally. I heard him telling lies when they asked about the women. He said that they were working for a month at the *trapiche*, the sugar-cane mill. The guerrillas said they did not believe him. Their leader fired shots across the river and went halfway across the bridge. He looked like a horrible ghost in the moonlight carrying a gun. Soon he came back to our side of the river.

I do not know why Gonzales became the butt of their jokes, but he was made to light their cigars, using a stick reddened in the fire. They laughed as he came to each of the guerrillas. I saw the glow on the cigars as they inhaled on them. Then Gonzales was dragged down to the hard, dry mud along the river bank. Two of the guerrillas pointed rifles at him. Gonzales began to beg for his life, but after a few moments they both shot him. His body twisted a few times and he fell over in a heap. My eyes widened in shock at the sight. I nearly cried out, but clamped a hand tightly over my mouth.

The guerrillas seemed to go crazy after that, threatening the others with their jerking guns. I thought they would shoot them all. I began to feel as if I would choke and lose my breath. The men knelt down and begged for their lives. One of the guerrillas started to laugh and said they looked like *sapos,* frogs. Another called them a bunch of young girls, along with other names that I will not repeat. Their wailing made me choke a sob that was rising from my stomach. I wanted to rush down and attack those thugs, but I knew that it would do no good.

Gonzales was then dragged out along the bridge. He was fastened onto the boards with thick ropes and left there. I crouched down on the floor of my tree house and forced myself to peep at him, hanging in the moonlight. I felt sick each time I looked. Finally, I lay down on my side with my arms wrapped around my head.

I must have fallen asleep, because I was woken by voices. It was bright outside. The guerrillas were near the bridge, arguing. Two of them were holding machetes. Gonzales was still hanging from the bridge. I could not see his face, but gashes and bloody bullet holes were visible in his head and back. One of the guerrillas walked out to the middle of the bridge and cut through the ropes that were holding him. Gonzales' body hit the water with a loud splash and disappeared. Then the body came up again and floated away on the river's strong current. I covered my eyes with my hands, trying to pretend that it wasn't really happening.

Around noon the AGRA thugs who had brought such evil to our commune left. They seemed to have lost interest in terrorising the men any longer. Eventually, as the afternoon grew less hot, the women and children came back across the river. Nobody said anything, but just stared in all directions, unable to believe how our peaceful lives had been shattered. When my friends came to call me down I could not move. I thought that if I stayed where I was and kept my eyes shut, maybe I would discover that it was all a bad dream. Mama called me but still I did not move. I lay on my back and told her to leave me alone. I stared up at the blue sky and thought of Papa and began to feel even worse. My throat was dry and my stomach ached a bit but I did not care. When it was nearly dark, Mama cooked some rice and beans and the smell of the food finally dragged me down from my tree. Mama said nothing, but folded her arms around me and squeezed me tightly. Her familiar smell made me feel a little safer.

Chapter 4

The following morning the adults drew lots, and different people took turns keeping watch, high in the trees across the river. Everyone was still very quiet, each lost in their own thoughts. Paul Rooke asked me to start a soccer game with the other young ones while the adults talked and prepared a communal meal. Our game of soccer was very tame. There were none of the usual disputes about offside goals or handball decisions. Once my side claimed a penalty, and the girls and boys on the other team agreed. When our side scored, instead of making a hullabaloo over the scorer, we just placed the ball in the middle of the two teams and carried on with the game.

The meal was like the banquet that we usually had on *el dia de navidad* (Christmas Day). There was *cuchucoa* soup with corn, potatoes and delicious pork; *frijoles* and *plátano* – red beans and fried green bananas. The adults talked in hushed voices but there was none of the usual discussion. The atmosphere made me more nervous. Other things were even stranger – there was no alcohol drunk with the meal; there was no music, singing or jokes; there was no dancing afterwards! When Martha pulled a funny face, instead of getting a laugh from the adults she was scolded.

After the meal we were sent outside and the people on lookout were changed so that they could eat. I went with two others to feed the chickens and the horses while the men unloaded the truck that had been hidden. I went to be with El Dorado. He was the only one who looked normal to me. I stroked his nose and whispered in his ear about what had happened. When I came back to report that I had done my work the adults were having an argument.

'Pepe is too young for such a task,' Mama was saying to everyone in the communal hut.

'We must work together in a time of crisis,' Paul Rooke replied in his booming American accent.

'You saw what happened to Gonzales,' Greta put in with an angry look at Mama.

'You will help, Pepe,' said Hank Shepak, pushing a finger into my left shoulder so hard that I nearly fell over.

'I am sad about Gonzales,' I mumbled. 'He showed me how to make a sling and shot.'

'Gonzales could take down a bird from the sky easily,' Hank said. The adults smiled in remembrance and then became silent.

I talked to Mama afterwards, but she seemed worried and anxious. What was this task that they had for me? All my questions went unanswered. Instead she weighed the air with her hands and walked away from me, wanting to be alone. At sundown, the women began to pack up their bundles and baskets, ready to go across the river again and hide, while the men loaded up the truck with the remaining tools as they had done every night since the attack by AGRA. I didn't have to help along with the other children because of my special mission. But what was it?

I walked over to the fenced-off pen where the horses were. El Dorado shook mosquitoes off his face. In the last blazing sunshine of the evening he looked like he was made of living gold and his brown eyes seemed to burn. Whenever I looked at those eyes I felt strong.

I mounted his strong back, getting on by holding onto the tuft of hair between his ears and swinging myself up – at the commune we had nothing like stirrups, reins or saddles. Up high on the horse I felt like a king. I went for a short ride along the river bank and imagined myself riding to *Laguna de Guatavita*, the ancient lake full of gold and jewels. Afterwards I gave El Dorado a rub down and went to sit with the group gathering around the campfire.

After we had eaten, we sat watching the flames and us boys flicked pieces of bamboo in to make sparks fly upwards. It was a starry night and out in the vastness of space the Milky Way seemed to glimmer and sparkle like the special necklace that Mama wore on festival days. The lookouts were changed and then the women began to whisper goodnight. They climbed slowly across the bridge over the river, carrying baskets and bundles that contained blankets, sleep mats and some food. The smaller children stayed close by their mothers.

'Pepe, I do not want to make you afraid, since you have a long and dangerous ride ahead of you,' said Mama before she left, 'but look, there is a full moon to guide you.' Mama looked nervous as she spoke. I was nervous too, because I still did not know what my mission was. We both tried to give each other courage.

'If El Dorado is with me, I will be safe,' I told her.

'Pepe, I think I believe you.'

We hugged and somehow I felt that I heard Gonzales saying, 'Don't be hugging your mama too much. It will make a sissy of you.'

The men called me back to the campfire as I watched Mama walk away. She was the last to cross the bridge.

Chapter 5

'Pepe, this is your moment of truth. We have been your fathers, but now you must do something on your own which is both easy and difficult.' Paul Rooke spoke down to me with his hands in his pockets while the others stood around with their arms folded. He gave me detailed instructions: I was to take the commune's savings, the 'treasure tin', and ride with it to a secret tree, far away along the river bank. There was a secret rhyme I had to memorise that would lead me to the right tree. Paul and Hank made me say it back to them over and over until they were satisfied that I had it right.

'It is a long ride, but you can be there and back before sunrise,' said Paul. 'Check that the tin is closed tightly, and use the chain and lock to secure it to a branch at the top of the tree. Smear the treasure tin and the chain with mud to camouflage them. Don't forget to brush away your footprints and the prints of the horse's hooves.'

Someone had made the treasure tin into a package with a rope attached that could go over my shoulder and upper body. Mama had left me some *taguas*, or ivory nuts, for El Dorado and a food parcel for myself of bananas, kidney beans and a few corn cobs. All of this was wrapped in a cloth like a bandana that went over my head and across one shoulder. The men also gave me a water bottle attached to a belt that went around my waist.

When I put on my gear I wasn't able to mount up. El Dorado seemed to shy away, perhaps because I clanked and thumped as I moved. On my first attempt, I fell back and one of the men caught me. Then Paul steadied El Dorado, making clicking noises with his tongue. He held the horse's head while Hank made a step of his joined hands and I mounted with ease. I felt great looking down at everybody.

'You know why it is you who must go?' Paul narrowed his eyes, drew on his cigarette and exhaled smoke.

'No,' I muttered, a blank expression on my face.

'The guerrillas know how many men there are in the village,' he explained. 'If they come and one is missing, they will be suspicious.'

Hank made a fist with his hand. 'Courage, Pepe! Someone will go and get the tin when the situation with the guerrillas has improved. But they mustn't get their hands on our treasure. We are depending on you.'

'You won't forget the secret rhyme?' said Paul.

'No, I will remember.'

The two men looked at me seriously, as if weighing me up. Suddenly, Paul shouted, 'Hold on tight,' and he slapped the horse on the right flank, making him bolt forward. I had no time to say goodbye as El Dorado, with ears forward like two fins, galloped onto the moonlit river-bank pathway. This path was wide but muddy, and overgrown in places. It had been cut many years before I was born by a lumber company.

I had a long ride ahead of me, but I was glad I had El Dorado for company. I thought of the ancient Muisca Indian warriors, and felt a bit braver. I gripped the horse tightly with my legs and leaned forward, holding onto his hairy tufts with my fists for dear life. 'Come on, El Dorado, we can do this,' I whispered. He snorted a reply.

It was late August and the night was warm after the torrid day's heat. I was glad that the moon was bright in the sky. The river glittered like dull silver to my right, while the jungle to my left looked like a vast black wall, impenetrable and endless. In among the vegetation and trees, I knew that all kinds of creeping animals and insects stalked each other.

The path I rode along, dark grey in the moonlight, seemed to snake its way up to the sky, where the stars glowed on El Dorado and me, and our secret mission. I had to concentrate, to urge El Dorado steadily on, and to watch for obstacles, dark shadows that hid gnarled and twisted roots or sharp rocks that he could trip on. I couldn't think of Mama and the others, of whether AGRA would return and cause more evil. I recited the secret rhyme to myself, to keep me calm:

Where the river's bank was washed away
There's a knuckle of rocks and buriti trees.

Go there at night but never by day;

The tree is three by thirty-three.

El Dorado began twisting his neck to one side as we galloped along. He sensed something up ahead, something I couldn't make out yet. I inhaled deeply and my whole body tingled with nervous excitement. Then, as the path widened to a sandy expanse, I saw them – a score of basking crocodiles, like long tree trunks, lying across the path. They all turned their heads to look in our direction as we approached. Their spiked backs, protruding eyes, long snouts and tails glistened wetly. El Dorado began to slow up. He snorted and shook his head. Was he afraid too? No, this was a signal to me to shout and make noise. We must not stop, El Dorado was telling me.

I gripped the horse even tighter – now was not a good time to fall off! I shouted at the top of my voice, giving voice to all of the tension and grief of the last two days. El Dorado whinnied loudly, sounding like some terrible monster from the depths of the jungle. The moon seemed to stare down on us in surprise. Some birds were startled and they flew off, rustling leaves and foliage and hooting at the disturbance. The noise we made must have scared one of those hoary crocodiles, and the rest followed. Like a herd they began to shuffle on their small, webbed legs down towards the river bank. El Dorado veered behind them and then we were past them. We galloped furiously along for a short while, then slowed to a steady pace.

We rode on until my whole body ached with exhaustion. Finally, I spotted what we were looking for – three huge knuckles of rock, like a giant's fist pushing up out of the earth, stuck out of the mud of the river bank, and just beyond was a small grove of buriti trees.

Where the river's bank was washed away
There's a knuckle of rocks and buriti trees.
Go there at night but never by day;
The tree is three by thirty-three.

I dismounted in a giddy state, my feet somewhat wobbly on solid ground after the long ride. My hands shook from having clasped El Dorado's mane for so long. I checked the treasure tin, and breathed a sigh of relief – it was still secure and the food belt was intact. I unrolled it and ate a handful of seeds, then bit into a piece of corn. El Dorado looked down at me and shook his head. I gave him some of the ivory nuts and brought him to the river's edge where he had a good, long drink. I opened my bottle of water and tilted my head back. I don't think I was ever so thirsty, and gulped down great bellyfuls of the cold water.

'Well, El Dorado, so far so good,' I whispered.

Chapter 6

I checked the tin strapped to my ba[   ]
then turned to face the dark shadows of [   ] was
in total silence, as though all of the night c[   ]es were
holding their breath. I half expected the quiet to be suddenly shattered by the jeeps and loud music of the AGRA
guerrillas, and as I thought back to the horrible murder of
Gonzales a knot of fear settled in my stomach.

'Okay, Pepe,' I told myself, 'you must march into the
jungle now. El Dorado is here to help.' According to the
rhyme, the treasure must be hung safely up a tree that
was three times thirty-three paces away from the giant
knuckle stone. Of course, they would have to be large
paces for me, because the rhyme was written for an adult.

I clenched my fists by my sides and began measuring
the ninety-nine paces to the secret tree, always looking
straight ahead and ignoring the strange hoots and shrieks
from the forest's depths. I could hear El Dorado following, always a few paces behind me. When I got to
ninety-nine I felt something magical must happen, but I
found myself face to face with a clump of leafy vines. I
had to return to the rock and start again. On my third
attempt, counting my steps slowly and keeping each

ast, I was in front of a great, silent
black in the moonlight. This was the com-
secret tree, and a grin spread over my face as I
gazed up into its branches.

The climb would not be easy. The tree's first branch
was well above my head – I could barely touch it, even
standing on tiptoes. Suddenly I felt weak at the thought
of getting up to the top of this tree. I willed myself to be a
bird but, of course, I could not fly up. Instead I took a few
deep breaths and leaped up at the branch. After much
huffing and puffing, on one of my better leaps, I got both
hands on it, and managed to hook one arm over it. I
hauled myself up and hung over the branch. El Dorado
was staring up at me with a confused look.

I cursed Paul, Hank and the other adults – this was a
climb for a man, not a mere boy. My knees were wob-
bling as I carefully grappled up to the second branch.
'Don't fall, Pepe,' I told myself over and over. But the
branches were closer together now, and it was easier to
climb. When I judged that I was high enough, I sat on a
branch with my back resting against the trunk. I felt like
the king of the jungle, looking down on the dark forest
floor.

I chose a good, strong branch to tie the treasure tin to.
The tin had rings of metal at both ends and, after checking that the lid was screwed on tight, I laced the chain
through these. I wound the chain around the branch a
few times, then climbed carefully down for the lock that

was in my food belt. I could hear Paul Rooke's voice in my mind. In his big American voice, he seemed to be saying, 'You are responsible for over ten thousand in banknotes, kid!'

I jumped down off the last branch, then stared up into the darkness to see if the tin and the chain were visible. I couldn't see them, but it was hard to tell in the black shadows of the great tree. Next, I rummaged through my gear for the lock, a heavy brass one, and put it my pocket. What food was left I emptied out of the *bandana* and spread on the ground. I scraped down into the mud by the river's edge and got out handfuls of damp stuff, making a little pile on the cloth. Then I folded the *bandana*, and tied it again around my shoulder.

This time the climb was not as difficult, once I had scrambled onto the first branch. The tin and chain dangled safely from their branch, and I sat above them balancing against the tree trunk. My hands shook a little as I snapped the lock shut on the chain. I caked mud all over the tin and chain to disguise them, then sat looking at my handiwork. I had done it! Our treasure was safe from the guerrillas.

I descended slowly once more. Then I found a branch with a wide fan of long leaves. I broke it off and dusted the lanes of footprints we had made. I was exhausted now, and I noticed that El Dorado's head was flopping, but we couldn't rest here. I led him away from the treasure tree and back along the bank of the river. A little way on, two over-towering trees made a natural gap into a mound of ferns and we came to a halt amongst them. El Dorado went down onto his knees and then keeled over, resting his thick neck on the ground. It would not be long until deep snores came from him. This I knew would keep small animals away and make bigger ones wary. I snuggled in near his head, putting my arms around his neck to share the warmth from his body, and rested one cheek against his head.

Chapter 7

I must have fallen asleep instantly, and when I woke it was still night time. The moon had moved to the other side of the sky. I was cold and stiff, but I felt proud when I thought of what I had done that night. We both stood up and El Dorado shifted restlessly, sniffing at the dark trees in all directions.

I mounted, feeling like a great Muisca warrior who had completed his mission. El Dorado soon broke into a gallop and I held on tightly. I felt that I had grown up that night. I was no longer a small child, playing foolish games.

But the night was not over. As we galloped along I began to wonder if I would recognise the village in the dead of night. I had never been this way before and I worried that I might ride straight past the commune in the darkness. Surely El Dorado would recognise his home, I told myself, but what if he did not?

These thoughts occupied me as we rode alongside the vast sweep of the river. We rode for a long time, my impatience growing steadily as I saw no sign of the village. The horizon was turning brown as the sun got ready to rise for another day. Then my eye was drawn to a red glow in the distance, too narrow to be the sun below the horizon. It looked like the illumination that you see at night when approaching El Encanto, the town near us with electric streetlights. Was it a small town ahead? How could we be so lost when we were following the river? I was beginning to panic, but El Dorado kept galloping along. At least he seemed to know where we were going.

As we drew nearer I realised that what I saw was a fire. The commune was on fire, enormous orange and red flames leaping into the sky. My first urge was to thud my feet into El Dorado's sides to goad him on with greater speed. I had only one thing in mind, to get to the village quickly. El Dorado had other ideas though. When we were close to the commune, he took us in a curve off the trail, away from the river and up through the jungle. We came out behind and above the village, so that we were looking down onto the disaster. I don't know whether El Dorado was fleeing from the flames or whether he sensed danger that I couldn't see, but either way it was fortunate that he took over.

I saw the huts in flames, a circle of burning stacks, the larger communal huts making bigger cauldrons of flame, crackling, spitting fire and belching smoke. The sharp, acrid smell of burning added to my fear. Of course our huts, so fondly built, easily made blazing fires – this I saw for the first time in my life.

The AGRA thugs were down by the river bank, taunting the men from the commune with guns and passing around bottles. I couldn't see Mama or the other women or children. At least they had got away! They must be in hiding across the river. The men were standing very still, not saying anything for fear of angering the guerrillas. Each guerrilla swayed as he gulped from a bottle or swung a gun around. The jeeps were there, their glaring lights making the scene even brighter. There were fires on both sides of the river – they had set our wooden bridge alight. It had broken in two, and hung down into the water, but the scaffolds that supported each end were blazing brightly.

I was siezed with a fierce anger, but what could I do? I patted El Dorado with a limp hand, staring unmoving at the flames. We stayed like that for a long time, until I saw that some of the guerrillas, those angry apes, were stumbling over to their jeeps. They were obviously very drunk, and soon they were all asleep, sprawled in the seats or across the backs of their vehicles, except one who sat under a tree near the river with a rifle laid across his lap. The guerrilla who was keeping watch lifted his rifle now and then and fired a single shot. I thought this would wake the others, but they didn't move a muscle – they must have been very badly drunk.

El Dorado was becoming agitated and snorted as if to say, 'Well? What are we going to do?' Suddenly I had a daring idea. I could see that El Dorado was angry with the lookout who held the rifle.

Looking back, I can see that courage is a thing of the

moment. If thought about for too long, fear and hesitation return and nothing can be achieved. I whispered to the horse, 'Okay, El Dorado, we are going to catch that ape.'

We moved carefully down in the dark shadows of the trees and began walking silently to where the scaffold of the bridge still crackled with fire and flame, giving off that sharp smell that makes horses restless and alert. I heard the men making bird noises to catch my attention – they had caught sight of us and were warning us to stay back. But we had to take a chance on it.

'El Dorado, you could take that guerrilla like a carrot from the bunch,' I whispered into his ear. He began to lurch in all directions, making him difficult to hold. I took a deep breath, then put two fingers into my mouth and whistled right into his ear. El Dorado shot off and struck like lightning against the man with the rifle. That guerrilla never saw the horse coming. To my delight, one thud of El Dorado's head into the man's side was enough to knock him flying. He fell over and his rifle was flung to the ground. We swung around quickly and ran back into the shadows.

Hank Shepak was quick to act. He recovered the rifle, cocked it and rammed the muzzle into the guerrilla's neck as he lay on the ground.

'¡Que burro! Tranquilo, hombre,' Shepak said to him in his basic Spanish – 'You ass! Keep quiet.' The other men grabbed the guerrilla roughly. Someone took off the *bandana* from around his neck and stuck it in his mouth, in case he might shout. I jumped off El Dorado, who must have injured himself in the assault, for he limped and there was a slight bleed from one of his nostrils.

I peered out through the trees at the terrible scene. There was very little left of the commune by now. Our village looked as if it had never existed. But now the tables had been turned. Hank was armed. He looked like a guerrilla himself in the brightening dawn.

I cannot say that I clearly saw the shooting. I know that the men got some more rifles by force from the AGRA thugs. There was use of some machetes also, those sword-like knives. There was a lot of shouting; jeeps revved up and crashed. One was pushed into the river, and it quickly filled with water and sank.

In the end, as with any battle, there was much death. I do not want to describe the horror of it. Three men from our village were killed in all the confusion. I had known them all my life. Five of the guerrillas were killed, three others shooting their way out of the battle and making off in one jeep, swearing revenge. Others ran off into the jungle. The man that El Dorado knocked to the ground was butchered with machetes. That was not a pretty sight.

Then it was over. In the raw morning light, the men stood around surveying the carnage. Five men in the commune now held weapons. The women began to shout from across the river, trying to make themselves heard. Mama was frantic until she saw me walk out, lead-ing El Dorado. I raised my arm in salute to her. It was going to be a very sombre day, and the beginning of a period of grieving for loved ones.

All that morning we launched the raft out across the river and back, bringing the women and children across in twos and threes. When they were all safely over, a communal meal was prepared and everyone who felt up to it ate hungrily. There was very little talking, although some of the men kept telling me that I had been very brave. 'Crazy, but brave,' is what Paul Rooke said.

The next day we buried our dead with a display of flowers, incense, chanting and ceremony that had been used for kings in the olden days. There was no ceremony for the bodies of the guerrillas – they were simply shoved into the river. 'Food for the crocodiles and fishes,' I heard Hank say. With our new store of weapons there came a sense of security. One of the abandoned AGRA jeeps was found to contain a box of ammunition.

The work on rebuilding the commune was delayed because of arguments among the adults. Some wanted to put the new huts in a different location. Others did not. Mama had a completely different plan.

Chapter 8

It took many days to saw wood for the new huts and a new bridge. In the meantime, everyone slept under rough shelters of woven branches and leaves, while a few of the men took turns to keep watch for AGRA. The five guns were our safety, even though the use of violence was against the principles of the commune.

I found the rebuilding of the bridge exciting. The activity helped me to forget the awful events that had happened. One of the men rode on horseback to El Encanto for rope, nails and pulleys. All of this was paid for on credit. The commune had decided not to touch the store of banknotes that I had hidden in the secret tree. They wanted to live on credit in case word got around that the commune had large sums of money. Everyone worked long hours, sawing, measuring and nailing, and soon the bridge was finished.

From now on, I slept in the big hut across the river with the women and other children. The men stayed on the commune side every night and were quite brazen now that they were armed. I was yawning one night as I slouched towards the bridge when I heard the men say that if the guerrillas came they would meet heavy resistance. If necessary, a retreat would be made across the river for the extra hidden supply of ammunition.

Work began on rebuilding the huts. It was decided after much discussion, and some arguing, among the adults to move further away from the river, up onto higher ground. We had to work hard, because everyone was quickly growing tired of living without a proper roof to shelter under. El Dorado and the other horses helped with the work too, hauling poles and branches.

Each hut began with a tall central pole, surrounded by a circle of poles about a third as tall. The roofs sloped down from a high point and were packed with layers of leaves, fastened until they were watertight.

One evening Mama told me quietly that she was waiting to pluck up the courage to announce at the next meeting that we would leave the commune. We were going to go to live with my grandmother, Mama's mama, in Cali, a big city on the other side of the country. Something had changed in Mama because of what had happened, because of all the violence and death.

Then, one night, AGRA came again. I was lying on the floor of the big hut with the women and children, waiting for sleep to come, when I heard the rumble of jeeps coming along the river. None of us moved; none of us even breathed as we listened to the guerrillas approaching. We heard shouting and a few shots being fired, and then the noise stopped. The women grabbed at us in case we would make a sound. I was pinched in the arms and my mouth was grabbed – as if I would blurt out a word! The faces of the women remained as still as stones and anyone who tried to whisper was chopped at with someone's hand. What had happened?

We crept out of the hut and over to the edge of the trees as far as we dared go, for fear of being seen by AGRA. It was a dark and murky night without a moon, the sky backlit with stars. Occasionally I could just about make out the shape of a gun, or one of our armed men changing position. Suddenly we heard a lot of shouting, and then the shouting faded away again.

Then the headlights of one of the guerrillas' jeeps were switched on. Their leader walked out into the light with his arms raised as though to embrace a friend. One of our men walked out to meet him. It was Hank Shepak. The two men stood talking as if they were having a friendly chat. They talked for a long time. The guerrilla leader produced two cigars and they both smoked. I yawned into my hands and tried to rub the sleep from my eyes as I watched. What they talked about I do not know, but no more shots were fired.

Eventually the guerrillas all returned to their jeeps. They revved up noisily and sped off into the night, the engines becoming no more than a purr of sound in the distance.

After a while Hank crossed the bridge, holding a lantern in one hand and a gun in the other. We mobbed him and at first he sniggered, speaking in Spanish in his funny

American accent, *'Tranquilo,'* which means, 'Take it easy.' We followed him back across the bridge to the commune side, and everyone listened as he told us about the truce he had made with AGRA. We would have to give a certain amount of our produce to them, and help with harvests when they hired migrant workers. We could keep the weapons that we had taken and they would generally leave us alone. A lot of the women nodded, looked at each other and began hugging their youngest children. But Mama gave me a look which made me shiver. She looked across at Paul Rooke and he gave her the thumbs-up sign.

'Not a bad deal, eh, Maria?' Paul bit his lip as he asked Mama's opinion. 'I think Hank has struck a good deal with those guys. Now we can get on with our lives.'

'You call that a good deal?' Mama yelled at him. 'We will be slaves to those AGRA ___' She used an unrepeatable word which made my ears go red.

'Look, it is only like paying some tax.' Hank tried to calm her down. 'Anything for a truce and no more killing.' He looked around for support, and some of the others nodded in agreement.

'Pepe and I are leaving,' said Mama flatly. 'Whatever I am owed from last year's work can be cancelled, if I can have enough money to travel to Cali.' I grabbed at Mama's arm and looked up at her. I wanted to speak but she clamped a hand over my face to keep me silent. I had known for days that she was planning to leave the commune, but somehow I didn't think that she really meant it. I could think of nothing but the opposite of what Mama said. This was our home! To leave seemed wrong, horrible, crazy, but because I was twelve years old I had no say in the matter.

The grown-ups argued for a few minutes. My friends looked at me expectantly, hoping that I could somehow change Mama's mind. Then Hank hushed everyone and promised that she would get the money. He reached out to shake her hand.

'I will never shake hands with a friend of AGRA,' Mama shouted at him.

Chapter 9

We had a long distance to travel – from where we were in the southeast of Colombia to a city many miles away, in the west of the country. It was possible to go by boat along the Río Putumayo but Mama was advised against it – it was too expensive for us and it would still leave us with a long journey by land to Cali. Boats could also be attacked along the river at docking stations and there would be other difficulties that the adults discussed with Mama.

Mama decided to wait for the 'loner' of the region, Jairo Alzate, a strange character who occasionally visited the commune. He usually stayed only one night before moving on. He always frightened us children a little with his stories of the ghosts and monsters of the mountains. But he was a good guide, as he knew every path and road for miles around.

Jairo came to the commune a few weeks later. He arrived late at night, so I did not see the 'loner' until the next morning. He was talking to the adults and smoking by the fire. He wore a *poncho*, a garment typical of my country that is like a sleeveless coat, made of one piece, with a hole to put your head through. His black hat had feathers around the brim, his trousers were patched and his boots looked almost worn out. His two mules, which he looked after with great care, were tied up in the corral with our horses. He didn't say very much, but gave Mama and me a weak smile and nodded. When he took off his *poncho* he had various necklaces on underneath, including an ivory rosary with a crucifix that looked as if it was made of gold.

Jairo seemed very vague about what we wanted to do and agreed to everything Mama asked him. He refused to stay another night at the commune though – we would have to leave with him that evening. Keeping his gaze fixed on the ground before him, he said something about the phases of the moon, then began to draw in the mud with a stick that he took from the fire. I could see Mama was annoyed, but she knew that we would need Jairo for the first part of our journey.

Mama hastily gave away her utensils, her pots and pans and much of her clothes, but kept her jewellery and shoes. My belongings included my knife, a collection of river stones, a slingshot and my straw hat, which had men on horses made out of coloured straw sewn around the outside like a cartoon strip. I was very proud of this. There was even a guitar man on a horse, which Mama had sewn on. This was a memento of my papa, wherever he was – the man who did not care for me, as father bird does not care for last year's nest, Mama once said.

We put our possessions into an old carpet bag which

had been used by so many commune members that no-one knew who it belonged to, or where it came from. Whatever room was left in the bag we stuffed with food, and we brought a separate small crate of eatables for the journey. As evening came on I suddenly became very sad. My friends César, Jésus, Martha and little Jaime did not seem to know I was really leaving. They worked on with their parents, preparing food, as I rushed off to see El Dorado.

There he was with the other horses, eating from a wooden trough after a day of hard work. It wasn't a good time to visit. Like the others, he was hungry, thirsty, tired and a bit cranky. I approached from the front and he gave great lurching shakes of his head. As I tried to stroke him, he carefully stepped away from me. Only when I spoke, telling him my sad news, did he seem to listen and understand. He kept chewing as he stared past my shoulder, away into the distance. I wanted to throw myself at him and cling on forever. It was bad enough leaving my friends, but this was awful.

None of the adults wanted to say goodbye. They wished us a safe journey but they did not want to say anything about our leaving. I went for the last time to the huts looking for César, Jésus, Martha and Jaime. Their parents called out to me, *'Adios,'* while my friends walked out and broke into cracked smiles as they each gave me a hug. None of them said much; it was as if we had become strange to each other. They wanted to go with me but, of course, they could not. I had to say something, because we had spent our childhood together and had recently survived the attacks and the destruction of the commune.

'*Amigos*, we will meet again,' I said. '*Vaya con Dios,*' – which is the way we Colombians say goodbye.

'Some day you will ride back here on a big horse with your princess,' said Martha, teasing me because we had had many years of struggle together as boy and girl.

'Don't talk so crazy,' I said. 'The city will be noisy and dirty and the food will stink.'

'Oh no,' said César, 'you will like it.'

'Mama says I will have to go to school,' I told them, my face becoming grim. At the commune we had no schooling, except what the adults taught us.

We hugged in a circle, then broke up, giving as loud a cheer as we could for the future. I began walking towards the tree house for a last look at it, when I heard Mama calling me. Little Jaime held one of my hands with his two hands and would not let go. At first he laughed as if he could stop my departure. Martha grabbed his arms and unlocked him from me, and then I saw a big tear roll down one of his cheeks.

'He is so young,' she said.

I found it difficult not to weep as I left them. There was very little time to spend with El Dorado. I was able to hug him and sniff the deep, dark scent of his skin one last time. He flicked his tail off my head a few times and leaned against me, nearly knocking me over.

'El Dorado,' I whispered, 'El Dorado, I will always remember you. I will ride with you in my dreams every night.' Then I had to leave, because Mama was calling again, with greater impatience.

I helped Jairo to tie the carpet bag and the food crate onto the backs of his mules. Everyone had gathered around and was singing a chant to raise our spirits for the journey. My friends were at the front of the group, tracing bird flights with their hands. I looked beyond them to the horses in the corral. El Dorado made a dash for the gate and nearly crashed into it, stopping just in time. He kicked out his back legs, landing on them to hoist himself high on his hindquarters with a whinnying shriek through his nostrils and mouth.

'Come,' said Jairo gruffly, and we were off. I looked back a few times and Jaime was still waving. It was heart-breaking, so I did not look back any more. I had to walk fast to keep up with Mama as Jairo led the two laden mules off through the jungle.

'Pepe, we must keep up,' said Mama urgently. Of course, she was right. Without Jairo as a guide, we would get lost in the dense jungle.

Chapter 10

It was a very hot and sticky journey, along an almost invisible path. Jairo was always ten paces ahead with the mules, disappearing amongst the trees and bushes as we stumbled along, tripping over roots and slipping on wet leaves on the forest floor. We carried on like this until nightfall. Then Jairo, who had said nothing for hours, finally spoke: 'We will keep moving through the night, because we have the moon.' He turned away as Mama complained and we had to hurry to keep up with him. It got very rough as the dark plants and foliage brushed our heads and faces. However much we complained, Jairo remained silent as he walked ahead. 'He is more like a machine than a human,' said Mama bitterly.

After hours of this trudging along, Jairo stopped and helped us up onto the backs of the mules. He grabbed the halters and led us onwards. The sure-footed mules kept their heads down and carried us steadily onwards. Jairo kept pushing forward, never stopping, as though the trees were signposts and the spaces between them wide pathways. I could barely make him out and wondered how it was possible for him to move so confidently at night. He looked up at the pale moon and the millions of stars whenever the high canopy of trees was less dense. Once, a monkey shrieked far to our left, and Jairo chuckled as if it had told a great joke.

After a long time he spoke again: 'Do not sleep or you might fall.' This shook me out of my dozing. Later we stopped abruptly, making me toss backward, putting my hands on the flank of the mule to steady myself. 'Do not move. Do not speak.' Jairo's voice was a sharp whisper. Up ahead we saw what looked like hooded beings of a low stature, a line of them, bent forward and barely visible in the shadows. I thought I must be dreaming. At one point they passed about five metres from us and we held our breath. I do not know if they were people or monkeys, or spirits of the forest.

Before dawn, Jairo asked us to dismount and walk. Mama got cross with him, but he turned to her face-on and said, 'The mules have carried you for hours. They are carrying your belongings. You are carrying nothing but yourself.' To this Mama could find no reply, so we dismounted and walked on.

Finally daylight began to light up the jungle. Birds and small animals woke up and moved about looking for their breakfast, some on trees, others running or flying away from us. As the sun's beacon appeared at a low angle through the trees, Jairo found a cluster of low branches and grunted his approval. He unpacked the mules and they immediately lay down. We all fell into a deep sleep.

I woke in a warm sweat. It was some time in the afternoon, and teeming insects hissed and swarmed. Jairo's rifle lay by his side as he tended a fire, making small cakes of bread from tree starch. He pointed to some guarana seeds, white with brown rims inside crimson husks, lying on a big, green leaf. We crunched them down and they helped us to come alive. The bread was nourishing and Mama got some water from our food crate.

We loaded up the mules once more and Jairo led the way, heading in a direction that seemed to me to be as good as any. I had lost interest in where we were going and had to place all my trust in Jairo. Mama seemed grumpy as she walked heavily behind me. I turned to her and grinned encouragement. She shook her head and looked at the ground. A minute later I felt her hand through my hair and she patted me on the back.

We walked on through the rest of the day. As night was falling we were suddenly surrounded by a tribe I had never seen before. They were standing all around us, gazing intently. This shook us out of our thoughts and exhaustion. The men and women of the tribe wore beads and bracelets around the wrist and upper arm. Their clothes were simple loincloths, held with string at the waist.

Jairo made some hand signals and they lowered their spears as he moved towards them. 'Stay with the mules,' he said calmly under his breath, quickly covering the rifle in its saddle holster on one of the mules by dragging a blanket over it. Jairo smoked with the men and talked. He examined some of their weapons, nodding and smiling once when a young warrior showed him a knife. He bade them goodbye by raising both his hands to their raised hands.

We passed slowly through the circle of tribespeople, who stared at us and mumbled in low voices. Mama looked at the ground and I kept my hands by my side, so as not to alarm them. I noticed a boy about my age and a little girl, but I did not look at them. I was not afraid; I just thought that Jairo would want us to keep quiet.

We walked all through the night again, sometimes stepping over roots and fallen branches as though along the rungs of a ladder laid along the ground. We walked across rocks, up hills and around the edges of bubbling swamps. The night seemed to last forever, but finally dawn broke and again we slumped into a deep sleep, only to be woken for a small meal and then more hours of trekking. It seemed to me that I had spent my whole life walking through this jungle.

On the fifth day, though I had almost lost track of time, Jairo stopped as dawn came on. 'I will leave you here,' he said. 'I am going back.' He looked anxious for the first time whereas we, seeing the edge of the jungle not too far off, had lost all our fears. Mama protested, saying she did not know where to go next. Jairo sighed deeply and, without looking at us or saying anything, led on towards the edge of the trees.

We came out onto a broad hillside, a landscape without trees. The dim light of the jungle had suddenly opened into the splendour of a misty valley, a vast vista of horizon. It was as if we were about to enter another world. Mama began giving thanks to Jairo but he just nodded. 'Over there is Araracuara?' She pointed and he nodded again, taking our luggage off the mules' backs. We felt so happy that we began hugging each other. When we came to our senses we looked around for Jairo, but he was gone. The carpet bag and the food crate were on the ground, but Jairo and his mules had disappeared.

Mama and I were exhausted, so we stayed in the shade of the edge of the jungle and slept for a short time. When we woke Mama seemed anxious about the journey ahead, but I did not ask her what she was thinking about. I did not want to know what we were facing, in case my stamina would run out. I would simply keep walking, I told myself, until Mama said it was time to stop.

But when we had walked for what seemed like hours down the hillside, my feet were hurting and I began to complain. Mama curtly told me to keep up. It was dangerous where we were, walking alone, and we had better hurry and get to Araracuara, she said. I kept whining until she got very annoyed and shouted at me. 'You want us to go back?' she asked, her face strange and angry. I did want to go back, but I simply said, 'No,' under my breath, thinking she was cruel and heartless. We could never find our way without Jairo. I wondered why the world was so endless and began to hate it. Why couldn't Cali be closer?

We finally reached an uneven roadway and stopped, sheltering behind a large boulder to wait for the hottest part of the day to pass. Insects droned by as we slept fitfully in the heat. We woke, blinking up at the eternal canopy of the sky. Everywhere the long reaches of the horizon were shimmering in the heat of the afternoon sun. We were glad we had some water.

The road was badly levelled, stony and chalky, as we walked through the afternoon. Birds screeched as we passed groves of stunted trees. We came to a crossroads, where two skinny dogs lay panting. This was where we would catch the bus, and we sat and dozed off, taking turns to keep watch.

The bus came towards evening, tilting from side to side and raising clouds of dust. It stopped, letting off a noise like a gunshot as the suspension heaved and the engine throbbed. The bus was a *chiva*, the usual type of bus in that region of Colombia. It made me think of my papa, because we had travelled on a *chiva* when I was six, but I could not recall where we had gone.

This *chiva* was full, but an American backpacker gave Mama her seat. I sat on the wooden lid of the food crate, and leaned against the sloping back of a seat that faced in the opposite direction in which we were travelling.

I do not remember getting into Araracuara. I must have been asleep, because it was the middle of the night. An old man lifted me down onto the floor, away from his chickens that were in a suitcase with air holes. He was afraid I would fall asleep and keel over on top of them.

The next morning as I woke up, the bus was even more full of passengers. The noise of the people was awful as the sun rose again. Many were drinking wine, eating and singing to greet the sun. There was a guitar player. He was good, but I thought of my papa and felt glum. The driver was out of sight in his bay. The bus sometimes made sharp turns and some of the drunken passengers bumped over and back, bursting into loud laughter as their singing voices changed to weird tones.

After much twisting and turning, up and down hill-sides, the driver stopped the bus and stood up to address the passengers. One of the men went up to him, putting his arm over the driver's shoulder and poking him, asking him drunkenly to join in with the singing. The driver was bleary eyed from steering us along the narrow road. He raised his hands and the women called for silence. He said that he would curl up in his bay and get a few hours' sleep, because it was too hot for driving. He promised to get us to the next town – I did not hear the name clearly – by nightfall.

'That will give us a good view of the mountains,' one of the men joked.

'The hungry mountains,' shouted a woman from the back of the bus.

The windows were all open, but the air in the bus was stifling as we took our *siesta*. There was silence except for people stumbling in and out to relieve themselves under the trees. The driver slept for hours. He woke, went to relieve himself and then started the engine again. As he shifted the bus noisily into gear, some passengers moaned and snuggled up as comfortably as possible to keep snoozing. Hens and chickens crooned and clucked. I looked up at those who faced me, who were happily tucking into their picnic lunch.

We chugged steadily along the road until the bus came to a sudden halt. The driver shouted back to us not to move or say a word. There was a thudding on the door of the bus, and then some glass broke and fell onto the floor. What kind of passenger was this? Some adults started standing up but the driver bellowed at them to sit down on their fat bums and shut up!

In seconds, everyone knew what was happening. Nobody looked very afraid, just annoyed, as three armed guerrillas came on board. At first their faces were stern, but seeing us grow tense they began to smile.

'Greetings, friends and supporters of LOR,' shouted one with a black beard, dark eyes and a wide-brimmed hat.

'Ah, to be among our *amigos* is pleasant,' said another, who wore a red scarf around his forehead.

LOR *(Las Okupas Revolucionarias)* were a guerrilla group with less supporters than AGRA, as Mama told me later, but this only made them more dangerous – because they were a small group, they had to work harder to instil fear in people. We were certainly growing afraid on the bus, as they waved their battered-looking guns around. The driver was made to introduce the passengers to one of the thugs, and told to call him 'Captain'. Passengers had to give their names, and the 'captain' would greet them as if with respect and then look back to his comrades with an evil grin.

'Have you a small donation for LOR today, my fellow Colombians?' asked the 'captain'. 'We are working for your freedom,' he grinned, showing off his yellow teeth.

I had half-believed that they were actually friendly, but now I knew that they were not really working for us. *Las Okupas*, those blackguards, took so much from us poor people. Mama was frightened. They tore through the clothes in the carpet bag, grabbing a comb and a denim shirt. They forced two passengers to help them unload what they took from us all.

Next, everyone was ordered off the *chiva*. At first the driver refused to get off, shouting that he was responsible for the safety of his vehicle. The 'captain' persuaded him with a gun barrel, poking it against his ear so that the driver cried out in pain. We stood on the road, squinting against the fierce sun.

The roadblock was made up of their old, white Renault

car, along with some wood with barbed wire hammered into it and a stack of old tyres. I watched one of the guerrillas sorting the items stolen from us, as if he had been to the market. The 'captain' instructed the driver to open the gasoline tank of the *chiva,* and he stuffed in a cloth until it held tight. There was a piece still sticking out and to this he held a lit match. I was fascinated watching the flame flicker, until there was a small exploding sound. A bright sheet of flame leaped out from the petrol tank, lighting up one side of the bus. Everyone moved back.

The flames made their way inside the bus, and the seats caught fire. There were groaning and crackling noises, a stench of burning rubber and tin, and finally a loud explosion as the engine caught fire. Flames shot out from under the roof and the engine. The glass windows turned black and cracked in the intense heat. When the panes had shattered, the bus seemed to have shrunk inside the flames. There was smoke everywhere and a horrible stink of burning.

We watched as the 'freedom fighters' packed up their loot and put the roadblock materials into the boot of the Renault. They hooted and honked as they drove away from the burning wreck.

Chapter 11

I need hardly tell you how fed up everyone was, having been robbed and left stranded at the side of the road. After a lot of angry talk and cursing from the men and women, the driver organised a group to walk to the next town and send back a bus. He and six others walked away, leaving thirty of us behind.

A few of the men went to find wood for a fire. An old woman with a face like ancient tree bark produced a cooking pot and a frying pan from where she had kept them hidden from the guerrillas, under her enormous skirt! Soon, like magic, we were heating corn, rice and capers. There was a very small amount for everybody. Then we all lay around wherever there was shelter. I slept very little, watching the heaving bodies breathing in and out, and the noisy birds and insects around us.

Another *chiva* arrived at dusk, with a different driver. He chatted to Mama and tried to make her laugh. He also patted me on the head. We were allowed on the bus first and invited to sit on seats near the door, behind the driver's bay. When everyone was seated we set off again.

We were making great time on the road, as the adults

kept saying over and over. Late at night we stopped to eat rice and beans at a *cantina*, which was a welcome break in the journey. We didn't stay long though – the driver was anxious to get to Cartagena del Chiara, which is over halfway to Cali.

Not far from Cartagena del Chiara, the driver stopped in front of what seemed in our headlights to be rocks on the road. Then the rocks stood up – they were, in fact, two men wearing *ponchos*. They climbed slowly aboard the bus, their wide-brimmed hats pulled down over their eyes. They looked old and feeble under the dim roof lights. I thought they must have a fever, because an old woman behind us welcomed them and asked after their health. One of them nodded, a pained expression on his face. He produced a paper cup and got water from a family with a good supply in a plastic container. There was nowhere for them to sit except on the floor between the seats.

When we had got under way the men arose, produced guns from under their *ponchos* and held us up. They ordered the driver to pull the bus off the road. The driver replied that he would need one of them to assist him in steering. The bandit told him to do the steering himself, but the driver insisted that he could not steer off the road at this hour of the night, and would end up on the mud siding where trees sloped outwards. 'There is no automatic steering on this ship,' he bellowed, meaning of course the old bus.

The bandit pushed his gun into a side pocket and put

both hands to the wheel in between the driver's out-stretched hands. Suddenly, as if from nowhere, the driver had a pistol and he stuck it into the bandit's neck. He took the bandit's gun and held him hostage. It had happened so fast that everyone was amazed, including the other armed bandit who had begun his rounds, asking passengers for their valuables as if he were checking their tickets.

'Eh, pig,' the driver called to the other bandit, 'drop your gun or I will take him out of the equation.' The second bandit stood still, looking very foolish, not knowing what to do.

'Pig, I am serious,' the driver went on. 'I will make bacon of him. Drop it.'

There was a tense silence. None of the passengers moved. I watched while Mama joined her hands tightly as if she were praying. The driver asked again, and getting no reply from the armed bandit, held onto the hostage and fired one shot, putting a bullet into his leg. The man who was shot crumpled onto the floor, screaming and cursing. Blood flowed out of his wound, and Mama moved over, pushing me against the window so hard that one of my elbows began to ache.

'See, pig, I tell you no lie. I want your gun or I shoot him in the other leg, then the belly and finally the head. I have his gun. Are you blind, deaf and stupid? Don't you understand, pig?' The driver had got very brave. His face was less pale since he had fired the shot.

'Take it easy,' shouted the bandit. 'Come and take my gun.'

'Put it on the floor,' ordered the driver. 'One of the men will take it. Who knows about weapons?'

A man put his hand up and took control of the gun. The driver kicked the wounded bandit down the steps in front of the door, hitting his head hard off one of the railings as he fell. Then the driver walked along the bus and poked the other bandit in the chest with the gun, while the armed passenger, looking very calm, held the other gun with the barrel pointing at the bandit's head.

'Not such a smart piggy, are you?' The driver teased the bandit, leading him along the aisle and pushing him down on top of his comrade.

The next part is terrible. I do not want to remember it. I was glad at what happened to the bandits, but I can still hear their cries for mercy and their threats to get even with the driver. The passengers rushed to one side of the bus to watch as he pushed them out onto the roadside. Then the driver shot the second bandit, giving him a leg wound also. There was a lot of cheering and clapping from everyone. Someone brought the driver a water flask and someone else a slice of *tortilla*, or potato omelette. He started up the bus and we drove away.

Chapter 12

We drove through Cartagena del Chiara, and onwards for half the night. Nothing else bad happened. In the town of Florencia we were let down at the bus station. Getting off, I made a gun with my hand and pointed at the driver, who grabbed my finger and grinned. Mama thanked him, as did the other passengers, but he said, *'De nada,'* which means, 'It was nothing.' He said he was glad to be of service.

We slept in the bus station and next morning, after washing in the public toilet cubicles, boarded a long Chevrolet bus. It was a *'directo'*, a big bus with a printed sign saying 'CALI' above the front windscreen. The first part of our journey was very steep, up into the Andes, but at least there were no bandits or guerrillas. The passengers were clean, well-dressed people. Mama and I felt like beggars among them in our tattered clothes. We sat on the long seat at the back of the bus on our own.

After a few hours I got used to the mountain scenery, though I have to admit that the uphill driving, with all the gear changing and tight cornering, made my stomach ill. When we came down into a valley to cross a wide river, the Río Magdalena, I noticed that the roads were now very smooth. The bus moved evenly at a steady speed, with no bumping or lurching up and down. What a comfortable way to travel! Soon we climbed up another steep hill, and when we reached the top the city was spread out below us in a plain, backed by another ridge of mountains. It was an amazing sight – Cali at last.

We zigzagged down and down in the late afternoon sunshine and the vast grid of the city streets looked like a kingdom, with high-rise buildings and lights and noise everywhere. There were more cars, buses, trucks and jeeps than I'd ever seen. Then the view disappeared, as our bus was swallowed up by the city's outer suburbs. I squashed my face up against the window as houses, petrol stations, shops, phone boxes, banks and hotels flew by.

We walked for an hour to my grandmother Rosa's little two-bedroom apartment. My mama's mama, *Abuela* as I called her in Spanish, hugged me a lot, and offered us what food she had in her tiny kitchen. She was a plump woman, her silver hair tied up in a bun with a comb holding it together. Mama told her about our troubles at the commune – the burning of the huts, the shootings – and all about our long and hazardous journey. Grandma Rosa listened, hardly able to eat, her eyes wide with amazement.

'You could have been killed,' she kept saying, but when she looked at me she smiled, leaning across to squeeze me by the chin or tousle my hair.

After our meal we walked out into the streets. I felt so happy all of a sudden; gone were the jungle noises, this was the music of the city. There were so many people, all hurrying along in different directions, going in and out of the doorways of a thousand buildings. I could barely read the names outside the stores: Droguerías, Restaurante, El Café de la Bohemia, Banco del Estado, Hotel El Condor, Hotel La Paloma, Hotel de los Reys. I worried about getting separated from Mama and Grandma but I did not want to tell them – I also longed to be able to roam the city alone. As night drew in and more and more lights flicked on all around – in buildings, vehicles and all along the streets – I felt as if I was in a movie. Mama was excited too. She bought a newspaper called *El Espectador*. 'I wonder what has been happening in the world?' she said, laughing.

Grandma led us into a church. It was white and looked very plain, until you got inside and saw that the walls were painted with gold and lined with statues showing Jesus, Mary and many saints. Grandma put a few *pesos* in a tin box and lit three big candles, saying a prayer of thanks that we had arrived safely. Outside in the street, she laughed and said she was glad that we had come. She kept hugging us and we had to support her in case she might fall in the street.

'If you had been killed you would have gone into the easy life, and not have to work for a living,' Grandma joked and as usual rubbed my chin and tousled my hair.

Mama looked strangely at her but I decided that I liked this old lady, with her old-fashioned way of speaking.

Back at the apartment I was glad of a bath, as the water had at last heated up. Mama used the tub after me and then unpacked her necklace and other jewellery from the money belt concealed on her body. I went to sleep in a bed made up on the floor, but was awoken a little later by voices raised in arguing in the kitchen. I peeked in the door.

There were two cups on the table. Mama and Grandma were shaking and pointing at each other. 'If you can't find a job you can sell the jewellery. I will not be able to feed you and Pepe. I am barely able to keep my job chopping vegetables and washing dishes at the hotel.' Grandma's face looked red, while Mama's was white with rage. I sneaked back to bed.

Mama woke me in the morning and we went out, because there was no food in the kitchen except for pine-apple juice. Grandma had already gone to work. Mama went to one dealer after another trying to get a good price for her jewellery and in the end sold most of it. I do not know how much she got, but she looked sad. We shopped until we each had a big bag of groceries to carry. I felt like a rich kid with his mother.

When we passed a café Mama grinned at the aroma of coffee, ice cream and food, and we went in. We had a great feast. Down the street we found an internet café and sent two e-mails: one to the commune, and the other

72

to my papa. I had not heard from him since last *navidades* (Christmas).

Mama soon got a job at the same hotel as Grandma, cooking and cleaning. I was hardly allowed out on my own at first, except some mornings to Simago, the supermarket; then back to watch the television with Grandma – usually quiz games, soap operas and black-and-white movies that sometimes made her weep when the couple would start kissing at the end.

I heard Mama and Grandma late at night arguing about what to do with me. When I heard this I thought of running away and somehow getting back to the commune. I tried to remember the edge of the jungle outside Araracuara where Jairo had brought us.

Eventually, I also got a job at the hotel. I worked in the kitchen, washing dishes and enormous cooking pots. Besides the few *pesos* that we earned, we could usually get some leftover food at the end of each night. The *portero* of the kitchen kept telling us to wash our hands and we had to wear plastic caps to cover our hair. Some nights there was no food left over. So we went back to Grandma and she would usually cook a *tortilla* for us all.

Mama finally got an e-mail from my papa. She showed it to me up on the screen at the internet café. There were three lines in Spanish asking about my life; the rest was in English that I couldn't read. I begged her to explain the e-mail as we waited for it to print out. Sitting at a table, she had coffee while I bought myself some juice, carefully counting the change.

'I will tell you what he says after I talk to Grandma,' Mama said.

'Why?' I shouted, annoyed.

'Don't be such an old curiosity cat,' she told me.

I was told nothing, but had to listen that night as they discussed it. My ear got hot as it lay jammed against the door listening to them.

'Joseph is such a ___' My mama used awful language about my papa.

'Let the boy go. It is no life for a boy working in a kitchen. There is no future in that,' Grandma said.

'What do you mean? Do you think I like working there? I hate being a cook,' Mama roared.

'You are not a cook anyway,' Grandma said. 'You would have to go to school to become a hotel cook.'

They talked on and on, mainly about me, and that kept me listening. It seemed that I had grandparents in a country in the northern hemisphere. My papa's people. I knew they existed, but because I had never seen them they did not mean anything to me.

The next day when the van left the hotel to collect foodstuffs, I made sure to sneak on board. At the rear of the food market the driver saw me and I asked him not to tell on me. He said he did not care, so long as I did not steal anything. He just kept talking to the other men in the market and the forklift driver, who should have been loading up stuff for the hotel. It looked like the van would not move for a while, so I climbed out and started walking.

Ah, to be alone in the street! In the window of a shop called a 'travel bureau', I saw a map of the world. This was what I was looking for. Colombia had an arrow pointing to it, with a cartoon of a man wearing big sunglasses. When I went inside a man stuck out his tongue at me and made jokes to the young woman behind the counter. I told the woman that I was looking for my grandparents' country as I leafed through some brochures on the desk. The man got angry. 'Get out of here,' he said. 'Go to the library if you want to read.'

I asked an old man on the street how to find the library, and he gave me directions. It was a long walk, but when I got there the lady behind the counter was friendly. I asked her to show me a map of Iran, where my grandparents were. She opened an enormous book, and pointed out Iran on a map. There was a photograph too, of men riding camels across the desert.

Later, when I told Mama and Grandma about it, they laughed until they nearly cried.

'It was Iran,' I told them, 'where my papa was born?'

Again they howled with laughter. I stared at them, wondering why they were laughing at me.

'I am sorry, Pepe,' said Mama. 'You are not going to Iran.' She wrote the name of the country on the top of the cereal box for me: Ireland.

I went to the library again a week later, and the woman showed me Ireland on the map. It looked like a dog with a flabby ear and one eye which was a lake. It was a small country, surrounded by the sea. There were no deserts.

Now e-mails started coming from my Irish grandfather, Jack Carroll. It seemed so strange and exciting. Mama and I asked for extra shift work in the hotel kitchens in order to earn more money for my trip. I was impatient for my big adventure, but had to wait until we had saved enough for an aeroplane ticket. I also had to get a passport, and Grandma fussed over me, nearly pulling out my hair with a comb when I went to get my photograph taken. But our life continued very slowly and I felt I would never get to Ireland.

Chapter 13

One night Mama came back to the apartment late and she was in a good mood. She had got another e-mail from my grandfather Jack in Ireland. He was sending out money for my ticket using Western Union. Mama would have to provide pocket money for the journey.

'Pocket money?' Grandma asked, bewildered.

'Yes, "pocket money".' Mama translated the e-mail for her.

'But he has no pockets,' said Grandma.

'I know. I will have to buy him warm clothes,' Mama replied.

'Ireland is very far north,' Grandma worried. 'Will it be covered in snow?'

Grandma borrowed some money from people in the apartment block who were cousins of hers. One of them worked in a cinema, and he said that Ireland was full of snow and ice. All the people went about in long coats, with hats that covered their ears like Eskimos.

'Where will we get a snow hat in Cali for Pepe?' asked Grandma that night, combing her long, silver-grey hair.

'Where, indeed, in the whole of Colombia will we get a hat like that?' asked Mama, winking at me so that I would not pay any attention to Grandma.

'But I have a hat,' I said and got out my straw hat with the horses and men sewn onto it. I was getting worried now.

They bought me second-hand clothes. I got two T-shirts with car logos, a poncho, long trousers and a thick scarf. Grandma sewed earflaps onto my hat that could be tucked in, so that if I arrived in Ireland in a heavy snowfall I would be prepared for the worst.

'What about gloves?' Grandma asked. 'He might get frostbite, like in those American war movies.' She began to explain to me what frostbite was, but I did not understand.

'My cousin says there is a war in Ireland,' said Grandma, rushing into the flat one night. 'Are we sending little Pepe to his death?'

'There is no war where Pepe is going,' replied Mama evenly.

'Are you sure?' asked Grandma, getting increasingly flustered. 'How can you be sure?'

'I am sure,' said Mama. 'His papa never said anything about a war.'

The night before I left, Grandma put on the water heater for as long as she could bear to without thinking of what it would cost. I was meant to be the only person to have a bath that night, but Mama examined the water after me and found it still hot, so everyone had a bath. Then there was the problem of washing my towel in the bathwater and getting it dry by the morning. It was packed wet into a plastic bag.

The next morning, it was decided that we should all have some food at a café in the airport. I knew that Grandma would get weepy so I said, 'Why not stay in the apartment?' No, she wanted to come with us. She hadn't seen the airport since her honeymoon to Panama.

Mama carried the carpet bag to the bus stop. I carried the plastic bag with the wet towel in it and my hat. Our bus finally got to the airport through the crowded streets, and then I had two hours to wait for my flight. There were people rushing about in all directions, pushing trolleys and checking times. The carpet bag was labelled and taken away with other luggage. My ticket was checked at a desk, then Mama put it inside the back pocket of my trousers and buttoned the pocket closed. My passport was in my shirt pocket, which also had a button. My shirt didn't fit me very well. It was much too big, and I had to roll the sleeves up so that my hands poked out. I liked it though; I felt like a businessman going off to an important meeting.

We sat for a little while in the café. The drink in my paper cup was almost untouched. I felt lonely leaving Mama, who sat looking strangely small and staring down at the table. I would miss Grandma too, whom I had grown to love despite her crazy questions. They both noticed my mood and forced themselves to smile.

'You will have good luck in the northern world,' said Grandma. 'But keep warm. Remember to be careful. Watch out for frostbite!'

'You will send me e-mails?' Mama said.

'How long will I be away?' I asked, looking down at my feet.

'Well, Pepe, because it is so expensive to travel there, you should stay as long as you can,' replied Mama.

'But how many days?'

'Days?' they both asked. 'Weeks, months at least.'

Grandma wanted to use the toilet and got up, leaving us alone.

'Pepe, listen to me. I want to work in the hotel as a chambermaid and then maybe in the dining room. I will earn more money so I can move into my own apartment. I cannot live with Grandma much longer. She is driving me mad!'

'You two drive each other mad. What about me?' I asked. I felt miserable and suddenly did not want to go. Mama hugged me. It felt good, but there were many people at other tables and it made me embarrassed. I took up my hat and stared at it. Why had Grandma ruined it, by sewing on those earflaps? I would rather that my ears froze on the sides of my head in Ireland.

'Pepe,' Mama began and burst into tears. But soon she got a grip on herself and said in a squeaky voice, 'You have a lousy mother. And a lousy father.'

'Don't say that, Mama. You two are my only parents. Don't say anything bad about my parents,' I begged her, but this caused more tears to flow and then I began to feel weepy too.

Grandma came back and, seeing our sadness, tried to be jolly.

'I like the airport. It is better than a circus. And do you know, the sight of those aeroplanes beats any trapeze act, elephants and tigers. You've never seen a circus?' she asked me.

'Yes, I have,' I said. 'We all acted in our own circus at the commune.'

'Oh, don't mention that commune to me,' snapped Grandma.

Then my flight number was called and there was no more time for tears. It was a strange moment. I often picture it in my mind at night.

How do you say goodbye to your mother? You hug her. She tells you how much she loves you. And you know how much it hurts to love her, just at the moment of leaving her. I picked up my hat and the plastic bag with the towel. Mama was shouting something. Grandma was saying, he looks so small. I turned around and walked away, towards the queue of people waiting to board the aeroplane.

Chapter 14

My first time inside an aeroplane! The engines were revving like the sound of all the animals along the Río Putumayo. I was asked for my ticket by a smiling woman in uniform and shown to a seat. It was very comfortable.

The aeroplane soon started rolling down the runway, then it roared and began moving faster and faster. Suddenly we were off the ground. The other passengers looked very calm, talking quietly or reading newspapers, so I settled in to enjoy my first flight. I decided that aeroplanes must have been invented so that man could be more like a bird. It was such a thrill to be inside the belly of this huge metal bird, flying up through the clouds. We were given food and drinks, and the pilot's voice came through little speakers, saying it was a lovely sunny day in Bogotá, where we would land in two hours' time.

Getting off the aeroplane in Bogotá, I felt as if I had always been flying. My feet did not seem to be on the ground. I was in a kind of dream. One of the hostesses brought me to a desk with a sign: 'Lufthansa'. I was taken in behind the counter. Another hostess made phone calls and yet another hostess arrived as I was staring across the desk at the crowds of people. What a sight! It was a lot better than television.

We went to a room with a big conveyer belt, the 'luggage carousel'. The carpet bag with its label was going round and round until I grabbed it. The hostess led me on, through barriers and along corridors. Men looked at her and she smiled. To an air pilot she said, 'Meet my new man, captain!' They laughed. I clung onto my hat and the towel in its plastic bag while she carried the carpet bag. I offered to carry it, but she shook her head and smiled again.

I was left waiting in a lounge with airport workers in different uniforms. There was a television hanging from the ceiling, but it was showing news programmes and I couldn't reach up to change the channel. It was a relief to hear my name called at last. A hostess took me back out through the bustle and crowds for my flight to Zürich, in Switzerland.

It was a long way to Switzerland. We flew for hours, though I slept for most of the time. At Zürich airport I began to feel lonely. Everyone spoke a strange language, and seemed to be in a terrible hurry. Why had I left Mama and Grandma? Would I ever see El Dorado again? He was my only friend, the only one I could tell my troubles to. I wished I could go back to the commune.

Finally a hostess who spoke very bad Spanish showed me to where I had to go for my next flight. Soon I was in another aeroplane seat, waiting for another take-off. This time we landed in London. This airport was enormous, and even more full of people, but now they were speaking English, so at least I could understand. The hostess who took charge of me made me feel like a piece of baggage. She took me by the hand as we pushed through the crowd. I was annoyed.

Then we stopped. 'Do you like burger and chips?' she asked, showing her shining teeth in a big smile. I thought hostesses had some problem – they seemed to smile almost all the time. Their faces must get very tired! I was hungry, so I nodded and she got me a take-away in a cardboard box. I sat and ate at a plastic-topped table. The waiting in London went on for hours, until night came. I watched an awful lot of television and began to hate airports.

At last I was on the flight to Dublin on Ryanair! Not long after take-off we were told to prepare for the descent and then as we came down with a bump, slowing along the runaway, a voice thanked us and said, 'It is raining in Dublin – Ryanair can do nothing about the weather!'

I got off ahead of the other passengers and was shown along by a hostess into a crowded room. She soon spotted a man holding a piece of cardboard with 'Our Grandson Pepe Carroll' written on it. This was Grandad, a tall man with a beard and round glasses. He wore denims, a shirt and a jacket, and I noticed that he had soil on his boots. He thanked the hostess, praising the staff for escorting me safely through the various airports and then took a long look at me. He shook my hand very formally and then seemed to change his mind and gave me a hug.

'I like your hat,' he said as we retrieved the carpet bag. 'I have a bit of a hat myself in the jeep. You'll need it here in Ireland.' He grinned broadly. 'I bet your belly is hanging down? I mean, are you hungry? We could eat here at the airport. I do not like the fast food at all, but you might?'

'I'm not hungry,' I yawned. 'Just sleepy.'

'Right so, let's get you to the farm, and away from this mob. It's a lot quieter down in the county Meath. Pepe, I'm delighted to meet you and that you'll be spending some time with us. Your dad should be home from Canada at some stage.'

I took to Grandad immediately, and thought he would have fitted in well at the commune. His messy jeep – 'the crock' as he called it – must have been very old. A pane of glass on one side was missing and had been replaced with a sheet of polythene that flapped as we drove along. There were boxes, crates, rolls of plastic, egg trays, bamboo canes, two big balls of rope, tools and a brush handle in the back, and a deep, rich smell of vegetables.

We drove slowly for a while along lanes of traffic and I stared out of the window at aeroplanes landing and taking off against the night sky. The roaring of their engines made them seem like monsters waiting to swoop down on us. The city lights thinned gradually as we chugged along, with Grandad telling me about their small farm, and about the kinds of crops that grow well in the Irish climate. He showed me his hat too, a battered-looking fisherman's hat which looked a hundred years old.

We got to a place called Kells, and Grandad stopped the jeep with a big screeching of brakes and lumbered out. He returned with a comic for me, the *Dandy*.

'We can get you something better when you get settled,' he said kindly. 'Don't be surprised if you see me reading the *Dandy* myself.' I explained to Grandad that I could not read in English, only in Spanish. 'Ah well, you can look at the pictures anyway,' he said, 'and I'll ask your grandmother about teaching you a bit of English. Anyway, you can make sense to me, and isn't that enough to be getting on with?'

A short while later we turned off the road, up a bumpy laneway. We stopped in front of a little house, and my grandmother came out. She was a warm, plump woman with short hair, and she smelled of the countryside as she wrapped her arms around me. Her hands, like Grandad's, were coarse, with the shadows of earth in the fingernails. I looked from one to the other, at their bright, ruddy faces. I would grow to love these people. They worked on the land as I had, and it immediately united us.

'What is this?' Grandma asked. 'A towel, and it's damp? Give me that till I wash it and dry it for you.'

'Look, he has a better hat than mine,' said Grandad, pointing it out to Grandma.

They showed me my room upstairs. It used to be my

papa's, and still had some of his childhood toys in the wardrobe – a train set with lots of bits missing from the box; a spud-gun and a water pistol; books; a stamp album with three Colombian stamps – I was delighted. His camera had a crack in the casing. There was a radio without batteries, and a hurley stick that I thought was a boomerang at first. Best of all were the Airfix model aeroplanes and boats, most of them broken but still wonderful since they were my papa's. Three big jars contained seashells, marbles and old coins. On the walls were posters of pop groups and solo guitarists. No wonder Papa had gone out in the world playing music.

I heard Grandma calling me for a bath and she brought a towelled robe that had belonged to my papa. 'Give yourself a good scrub, Pepe,' she said. 'I hope you will be happy here with us. We are old fogies but we try not to be grumpy. You can tell me if you want anything special?' I wondered what she meant by 'old fogies'. She showed me the hot and cold taps, one with a red spot, the other blue.

'Grandma, I was born in the jungle but I'm not a monkey,' I said.

'Oh, you're able to crack a joke like your father,' she laughed.

I laughed too. I had never heard of anyone 'cracking' a joke before.

I was left alone in the quiet bathroom. It had thick bubble glass and outside it was pitch dark. I rubbed soap into my hair and played with the sponge, submerging it in the water and then squeezing it out over myself. Then I lay there for a long time in the hot water, wondering what would happen to me.

After my bath I got into bed and Grandma brought me some hot cocoa. It was sweet and delicious, but after one sip I was fast asleep. It was dark and I could hear jeeps coming into the commune and shots being fired. The guerrillas were back. My mother was shaking me to get up and run, but when I opened my eyes it was Grandma, with Grandad standing behind her.

'Are you all right, Pepe?' she asked, sitting down on the bed and stroking my forehead.

'You gave a shout. I think you must have been fighting a tiger in the jungle,' said Grandad. 'You're safe here. We have two dogs, Bran and Emo, and two cats, Max and Mojo. They're all outside keeping watch.'

Grandma stayed in the room with me, talking softly until I dozed off again.

Chapter 15

I woke to a damp, grey October morning. It took me a few moments to remember where I was, and then I jumped up out of bed and pulled back the curtains. With my nose up to the glass I had a view of the yard at the back of the house. There was a wheelbarrow with buckets in it. Behind a hedge were four goats. To the right was a small, stone outhouse and to the left another hedge. In front of this on a clothesline, my towel hung to dry among some other items. Some chance in this damp weather, I thought to myself. Where was the sun? The light outside was very dull. It looked cold. The hedge was a tangle of different types of leaves and thorns, an incredible weave of growth and colour. The few trees I could see had bronze and copper leaves that seemed to be shivering. I felt a bit of a shivering leaf myself.

Downstairs there were voices so I crept to my door, opened it and listened.

'There isn't a pick on him,' Grandma was saying, and she did not mean her favourite goat.

'He is small for his age all right,' said Grandad, 'and thin as a greyhound.'

'Well, I can fatten him up, but what will we do with him then?'

'He can help out. Sure, there's plenty to be done,' Grandad said.

They talked on about me. About my papa and mama. They had not a good word to say for my parents. 'Irresponsible' was what they called my papa. I would look that word up when I had a chance. Then I heard another word, one that I dreaded: school. It seemed that Grandma was a teacher, because Grandad kept saying, 'You can teach him at home,' but she did not agree.

'He cannot stay with us every day,' she argued. 'We can put up with each other, but why should he have to put with us?'

'I think he might like it. He's used to life on a commune and that is what we have here, sort of, a commune of our own.'

'Commune!' Grandma exclaimed. 'Are you cracked? We're not a commune! There are only the two of us. Can you not count?'

Her tone of voice was not cross, though. In fact, as I would learn, my grandparents never argued. Instead they laughed a lot, each making out that the other one was daft or going 'batty'.

I waited until it was quiet before I came downstairs. Grandma had gone to her class. She taught in a school for children with special needs in Navan, a big town near us, but further away than Kells. I had a chance to explore while Grandad was outside, washing some buckets in the yard.

The house was very old. Every ceiling in every room had damp patches and cracked plaster. The stairs wobbled and squeaked loudly. There were two windows in the long kitchen, an Aga cooker, a radio and a small television on a shelf above the door. Everything in the house seemed to lead into and out of the kitchen – the back door, a passageway leading to the front door, a downstairs bedroom, a scullery and a junk room with a computer.

The cats, Max and Mojo, were in the kitchen under siege by the dogs, which leaped up at the panes of glass on the back door trying to get in – I would soon understand that this battle never ended. If the cats were outside, the dogs were kept in. If the dogs got out, Max and Mojo had to run up the trees or onto the flat kitchen roof.

Grandad was nowhere to be seen when I went outside, so I had a look at a building that cast a dark shadow across one of the kitchen windows. This was a long, old shed with a red, galvanised roof. The metal door was unlocked, so I opened it and went in.

Inside it looked like a small science laboratory. It had two sinks, a freezer, shelves of jars, utensils, thermometers, round boxes and labels, all spotlessly clean. It was the cheese house, a place that Grandma would not encourage me to go into, because cheese-making was her special work. She even wore a white coat, plastic gloves, a hat and white wellingtons while working in the cheese house. I went out again, carefully closing the door behind me.

As I was walking behind the outhouses, Grandad called me. He was in the growing tunnel, a plastic tunnel that looked like a very long boat lying upside down on the ground. The door consisted of a sheet of polythene framed with wood. Inside the growing tunnel it was warmer. There was a narrow path along the middle to the other end and the roof curved down at both sides.

'Welcome to Fordstown Organic Foods,' Grandad smiled as I came in, shutting the door. 'FOG, they call us locally, among other names. Yes, your Grandma and I grow vegetables and herbs and sell them on to stalls in the Dublin market. Some shops in Trim, Kells and Navan take our produce too, but no supermarkets. Look: mushrooms, onions, beetroot, scallions, celery, herbs ... I tell you, we always have good soup. We also grow weeds, unfortunately.' He smiled.

'Wow,' I said. It looked like a lot of work.

'We are just a small grower. We also make goats' cheeses, yoghurt and bread, as well as growing apples and pears, and plenty of potatoes. Well, we cannot eat them all ourselves and I love to live near growing food – the aroma of it; the colour of it. It is called "organic" because we use no fertilisers. I collect dung and other mulch from all over.'

I spent the rest of the day with Grandad, as he showed me around – the field of potatoes, the neat little orchard of apple and pear trees. That evening I had done a half day's work when Grandma arrived home. She baked a wholemeal pizza, topped with peppers, onions, tomatoes, some of her goats' cheese, anchovies and chillies – they knew I would like chillies.

After our meal they got me to talk all about my life in Colombia, in the commune. At first I was shy and tongue-tied, as they sat silent looking at me. I felt as if they wanted me to stand up and sing a song for them. But soon I began to tell them about our last days at the commune. The attacks by AGRA. My ride on El Dorado to hide the treasure. The burning of the village. The shootings. My journey to Cali with Mama. It seemed to entertain them, and they listened carefully and asked questions, hushing each other every now and then so that I could continue. I began to enjoy telling my story. Grandma kept bringing out more and more food – apples, ginger cake, fruitcake, nuts and home-made toffee. It struck me that I would never go hungry in Ireland.

'What a wonderful little man you are to have made it through all of that,' said Grandma. She looked very impressed.

Then Grandad stood up. He almost had tears in his eyes as he went off to the junk room. He returned with a sea captain's hat, with a peak and an anchor. When he put it on he asked me to stand up.

'I salute you, Pepe Carroll,' he said seriously. 'You

have been in the wars. You have returned. When a soldier returns, he gets a pension.' Grandad reached into his tattered coat, took out his wallet and handed me a fifty-euro note. Wow! It was more money than I had ever had in my life.

'Yes, you deserve it,' Grandma nodded. 'Jack, why don't you help him e-mail his parents.'

Grandad wrote the e-mails for me, one for Mama and one for my wandering papa. I typed in my name and clicked on 'Send all'. Grandad said he would teach me more stuff on the computer and get some games for me.

Up in my bedroom I went through what remained of my father's toys and looked at the pictures in his story-books. There was one of a cowboy on a horse with a guitar! Finally, I tried to read the *Dandy,* staring hard at the words, but I only got frustrated. Suddenly I heard them on the creaky stairs.

'Oh, I'd say he's fast asleep,' I heard Grandad say. 'If you look in on him it might wake him up. Poor auld soldier.'

'You're right,' said Grandma. 'Well, I'll phone the school tomorrow. It's a pity we couldn't get him in locally, but the classes are all overcrowded. The school in Angerstown will be fine, though. Besides its only fifteen kilometres, twice a day. Do you think we can manage him here for the year, since his mother asked us?'

'It's only a year,' said Grandad.

'I know, but we reared our children long ago, and

even one turns us back into parents all over again,' muttered Grandma, puffing as she got to the top of the stairs.

I quickly put my light out and crept into bed. A year? What year? My mother was dumping me in Ireland for a whole year! I thought I was staying in Fordstown for a few weeks, and then going back to Mama after seeing my papa for a while. What was happening? Would anyone tell me? I began to feel helpless, lonely and upset. I cursed my papa and mama. But I would not cry. I would ask my grandparents about it in the morning. I wished for sleep to come, and eventually it did.

Chapter 16

I was grumpy the next morning at breakfast. It was Grandma's 'special' – porridge with a sprinkling of flax, sunflower, sesame and hazelnuts that she reduced to powder in a coffee grinder. Their milk was unsweetened soya. There was no sugar in the house.

Grandad came in from the yard dressed in his fishing hat, dungarees and boots, and carrying a handful of eggs. 'I couldn't resist when I saw the loaf of brown bread you made, with a hump on it like a railway bridge,' he said to Grandma. 'How's our little man?' He looked at me.

'I am feeling grumpy,' I piped up.

'Oh, why, Pepe?' They both stopped and stared at me.

'Oh, nothing,' I muttered, spooning my porridge into me, secretly enjoying keeping them in suspense.

'Come on. Out with it, soldier,' Grandad said, sitting down in front of a huge bowl of porridge and tapping his spoon into the palm of one hand.

'I am afraid to go to school, and ...' My voice gave out.

'And?' Grandma coaxed gently.

'How long will I stay in ...' Suddenly I felt I couldn't say, 'How long will I stay with you?' so I said, 'How long will I stay in school?'

They were very good about everything, and made me feel able to talk about my problems. They fully understood that I was missing my mama and papa. I must talk about it any time I felt lonely, they said. That made me feel better. And I could send e-mails whenever I wanted to.

Grandad was less strict about my going to school – he thought Grandma could teach me – but Grandma thought I should give it a try. 'Besides,' Grandad said, 'there's plenty to do around here. You can earn pocket money helping with the business.' He always called it 'the business', and answered his phone, 'Fordstown Organic Growers, Jack Carroll, can we help you?' Grandma thought it was a bit ridiculous and often called us from the fields, 'Will the Fordstown Organic Growers come in for their supper!' If she needed something picked from the polytunnel, she would call out, 'I have an order for Jack Carroll of the FOG.' Grandad printed his invoices on the computer and did his accounts from a folder on the desktop marked 'The Big Book of FOG'.

'I don't know how we'll fox your granny on this school situation,' he said later, as we weeded and hoed in the growing tunnel. 'You know, if you wanted to stay with us,' he said thoughtfully, looking like the 'king of three acres', as the villagers called him, 'I'd make you the boss when I retire.'

'But, Grandad, you told me you would never retire!'

'Well now, so I did,' he laughed. 'So I did indeed.'

Every Saturday that autumn we got up very early. Saturday was market day in Dublin and we would be working in the growing tunnel by the light of a halogen lamp before dawn. I was glad of my gloves as we packed carrots, parsnips, broccoli and potatoes from the sandy pit, along with celery, onions, mushrooms, apples and the all-too-precious pears. It was heavy work, hoisting the boxes into the back of the jeep. Then, after our porridge and a cup of tea, we would set out for Dublin with our 'treasures of the Earth'.

The growers met in a place called Smithfield, not far from the big river that goes through Dublin. The city early on a Saturday morning, with its bridges, castles, churches and countless streets sloping down to the Liffey, seemed a place for great adventures. Deliveries were easier than tending a stall at the market, according to Grandad. Our boxes would sell slowly, because Grandad was a small supplier. His customers were stallholders from various parts of the city. These buyers always wanted more and more when the produce was good. Sometimes Grandad's pears would not get a very good price, but he said that people had no taste for Irish pears. The cooking and eating apples sold better, but easiest to sell were the vegetables and potatoes.

With our business done, we would head for one of the cafés near the market for our weekly grill. Grandad was not really a fan of the 'Irish fry'. He would annoy the people behind the counter, asking what oil they used for cooking their chips and insisting that none of his food should be reheated in a microwave. I did not always understand why, but he explained that he was 'a bit of a health-food philosopher'.

'They'd fry the tea in that greasy spoon if you didn't keep an eye on them,' he would say.

Chapter 17

Saint Brendan's Technical School, Angerstown, in the south of County Meath, was my school and it was horrible. The school building was very old, with windows that rattled in the wind and long, dark corridors where the paint flaked from the ceilings. The tarmacadam covering the yard was crumbling and looked like a layer of coal dust.

My name made everyone laugh from the first day. The other children pronounced it 'Pee-Pee' instead of Pepe. All the local children seemed to know each other well, and hung around in various gangs and groups. Hardly anyone ever spoke to me, except to imitate my accent, which they thought was hilarious.

Our teacher, Mr Kermody, was nicknamed 'Crab' Kermody, because of the way he sat at his desk and stared without moving his head, and because of his slow, shuffling walk. He had curly, red hair, wore a cardigan with missing buttons, twirled his hands nervously and wheezed before speaking. His thick glasses made his eyes look like two tiny dots, while his teeth were broken and tobacco stained. His Adam's apple moved up and down on his long neck when he got angry, which was most of the time. He reminded me of a big, fat bird with his nasal, tweeting voice.

The boys and girls were reading really hard books, while I could not read anything in English. Metalwork and woodwork were a bit better, but I could not read the instructions off the blackboard in these classes either. When it came to history I knew nothing, because I had never been told about anything to do with the outside world at the commune. When did the Titanic sink? Who were the presidents of Ireland? Who was Saint Patrick? Finn MacCool? I knew nothing of the Great Famine, the Rising of 1916, the Great War, the Aran Islands, the All-Ireland hurling championship.

Everything was news to me, and this seemed to annoy my fellow students. They would ask me, 'Do you know what year it is?' Really, all I knew about Ireland was my U2 CD with the little kid on the front cover wearing a war helmet.

I felt like an idiot in class, but I couldn't pluck up the courage to ask Grandma to let me stay on the farm and work all day. At least I knew a bit about vegetables. But I knew she would not allow it, no matter how much I hated that school.

I soon had other nicknames – they began to call me 'Captain Colombo' after I mentioned escaping from the guerrillas in Colombia. I soon stopped telling anyone about myself.

I was also known as 'Peeper' Carroll. Oh well, at least

'Peeper' was better than 'Pee-Pee'. Other boys had nicknames too: Fishface Gibbons, Slob Nally and Frog Fanning.

On the drive to school with Grandad each morning we passed a group of caravans, parked together at the side of the road. It looked like a sort of commune, and there were even a few ponies. 'They're our native *tincéirí*, the Travellers,' said Grandad, 'the Joyces, the Tanseys and other families.' There were heaps of scrap metal piled up – old washing machines and fridges, parts for cars and vans. Like me, these people were outsiders. I longed to make a visit.

One afternoon, after I got home from my horrible school, I was kicking a ball up and down the yard. Grandad was going about his chores, inspecting our supply of potatoes stored in their huge crates in the shed. He came out with his glasses on, holding a thick notebook and his calculator. He was working at his 'sums', as he called the accounts, so I left him alone.

I looked out onto the road and, just then, a young horse came galloping past, obviously distressed and frightened. She was followed by five Traveller lads, running at full speed, trying to catch her. I took off after them, to see what was going on.

When I got to the village green the boys were in a group around the pony, trying to calm her down. Some local men were watching from the pub window, while a few others gaped from inside the post office. The

Travellers were throwing a rope, trying to lasso the terri-fied animal. I watched for a moment, knowing that they were doing it wrong.

'That's not the right way,' I piped up, but they didn't hear me. The pony shied and careered away from the boys, big lads in denims and stained fleece jackets, zipped up against the cold day.

'Come on, Starlight, stop all this messin',' shouted one of them to the pony.

'Don't ever rush a pony that has taken fright, lads,' someone called from inside the door of the pub. 'Go and get your father. He's the only one who can control that beast.'

'Our father is away in Kells,' one of the boys replied aggressively. 'We can tackle our own horse. We don't need the father.'

Three of the boys looked alike, short and stocky with flaming red hair. The other two were darker. I moved over behind the one with the rope, one of the carrot-haired boys, and poked him in the elbow to get his atten-tion. He twisted back to look for a second.

'What's up, doc?' he bellowed viciously, then turned to face the pony again.

'He is afraid of you and your brothers,' I told him.

'Don't be annoying me,' he said. 'Don't meddle with men's work. Do you know anything about the horses? Do you?'

'Yes, I do,' I said, fighting my nerves.

'I suppose you can spell "horse" and that's about it.' Carrot threw this back at me and kept his eyes on Starlight.

'I will show you,' I demanded.

'He'd knock you down with a kick,' shouted one of the others, but I walked out in front of them towards the pony. Just then I saw Grandad come onto the green. He stayed out of the way though, as one of our neighbours filled him in on the situation.

This was my moment. I knew that I had to ignore the crowd and focus on Starlight. She side-glanced me but still pranced rearwards. I put out a limp arm and began making clicking noises. 'Starlight, let me come over,' I said in a low voice. I turned to the Traveller boys and with a look, somehow got them to move back.

'Starlight, I'll meet you halfway. Come on, little pony. I can't hurt you,' I called out softly as the crowd went into an expectant silence.

I walked forward, making each step slower, more guarded, and keeping a low murmur focused on Starlight. If she rose up to attack me, I would fall back, and could trust the boys to rush to my support with shouts. Meanwhile, I advanced slowly, trying to gain Starlight's confidence, so that she would let me get closer.

And that is what happened. It may have looked like I was going into the lion's den, but really I was just showing a nervous animal a kind hand, something to calm her down. I kept reassuring her and it was not too long before she let me stroke her head and her mane, and rub her back. The crowd had the sense not to break the silence until one of the boys handed me the halter, out of sight of Starlight, and after more calming words I slipped it on her.

Leading the pony back towards its owners I felt like a champion. I saw Grandad out of the corner of my eye, biting his lip in relief and trying to conceal his widening grin.

Mrs Tansey, the boys' grandmother, known locally as 'The Witch Tansey', came over as a crowd gathered around. She grabbed my shoulders and stared into my eyes as if she was trying to look at something deep inside me. 'Listen, young fella, I saw something this day. You're made for the horses. D'you hear? Go off to the horses with you!' Her face was wizened, her voice sharp and I hardly understood a word of what she said, but they say that genuine witches can see into the future, and perhaps that is true.

Meanwhile the people all around the green cheered and clapped, and Grandad came over and put his hand on my shoulder. 'You had the heart sideways in me for a minute there, Pepe,' he said.

When we got back to Grandma, she was correcting school essays while waiting for a batch of bread to cook. She thought we had gone 'for a bit of jaunt' to Navan or Kells.

'Oh, my god,' she exclaimed on hearing about my

'taming' the pony for the Tanseys. 'Well, now, if they can't settle their horse and Pepe can, that is something. That really is something.'

'Oh, it's more than something,' said Grandad, beaming from ear to ear. He had a strange look in his eyes.

'What is?' I asked, confused.

'Yes, what?' asked Grandma, turning to face Grandad. She looked as lost as I was.

'Can't you see?' He laughed like a madman. 'You like horses, don't you, Pepe? Don't answer. You do, and they like you. That's it!' He clapped his hands. 'Why didn't I ever think of it before, especially when you told us about your adventures in Colombia?'

So I left them to it. Talking in riddles. Were they going to get me a job with the Tanseys minding the ponies? Hardly. But it must be something. Still, anything to get me out of that horrible school.

Chapter 18

I began to visit the Travellers on their halting site. Old man Tansey, the father of the three red-haired boys, let me ride Starlight bareback around the field. He had a broad grin with no teeth, and always wore a woolly cap on his head. Sometimes his mother, The Witch Tansey, came out of the caravan wearing her shawl over her head and pointed at me with one finger while the other finger pointed at the sky.

'I can see it all, sonny, both up here and down below,' she would cackle. 'At night it's up above for the likes of me to plainly see.' I had trouble understanding her a lot of the time. 'You're a horsey boy, but maybe your people don't know and you should tell 'em,' she would point and stare at me meaningfully.

I got on well with the Tanseys. They told me a lot about trees and plants, and how to predict the weather by watching the clouds and the way that birds change their positions in the sky. The boys showed me fox holes, birds' nests and places where rabbits and hares roamed. It was amazing how much they knew about nature, but they shook their heads when they talked about nearby towns and 'settled' people with all their houses, roads and cars. I was able to ride Starlight any afternoon I wanted after school, once I filled her water bucket and gave her a rub down. I sometimes brought her a few apples from Grandma.

Grandad had phoned a place called Abbeyvale House in Clonwell, County Kildare, and a couple of weeks later we set off after breakfast for a visit. I didn't mind where we were going, if it could get me out of my hated school.

CHASE, the school in Abbeyvale House, was a bit scary at first, with its big gates, long driveway and big, serious-looking buildings. There was a sign on the front of the main building which read 'Countrywide Horse Association Standards & Education'. Grandad had made an appointment and he went inside while I took a quick look around. There were a few horses in a paddock not far off. They were well groomed, lean and fiery-looking. I thought that if I mounted one of those creatures, we might almost take off for the stars. I could feel the energy and the power in them.

Through an archway out of an enclosed yard came three young lads about my age. They eyed me briefly without saying anything as they passed, each carrying a polished saddle, with metal stirrups attached by leather straps. They wore riding caps with goggles around the rims, breeches, jerkins with zips up the front and black boots, a bit like the wellingtons Grandma and Grandad wore around the farm, but

much better-fitting and far shinier. The three young jockeys had just been for a late-morning gallop, at least that's
what I heard them say.

I was in a trance staring at everything as Grandad
came over with another man. He introduced himself as
Paddy Deveraux, and shook my hand. A small, springy
man, he had been a jockey himself once, as I later found
out.

'So, you want to give us a try, Pepe? You rode in no
less than Colombia? The Colombian Gold Cup?' he joked,
looking me up and down. 'Well, now, you're grand and
wiry, like a greyhound.'

'He's a good steady fellow,' said Grandad, smiling at
me as if to say, 'this sizing up of you will not take long.'

Paddy Deveraux disappeared around a corner of a
building and called to someone, then returned to us.

'Ah, damn, I thought I'd get a horse for twenty minutes, but they are being fed and watered. It's buckets
and brushes, oats and hay at this time of the day.' He
glanced at the complicated-looking watch on his wrist.
It had little dials and buttons all over it.

'Listen, go up to reception' – he pointed and Grandad
nodded – 'You can get an application form and a bro-
chure there. You should really get Pepe to come here for
our open day in three weeks. Then he can get a mount
and show us all what he's got.' He smiled and was soon
gone around the building and out of sight.

Our talk in the Landrover on the way home never strayed

from one topic: horses. Grandad tried to think back to what his sister had once told him about the Carrolls and horsemanship. 'While I can hardly say that any of us was born in the saddle, I think we had at least two ancestors who went to the races and the dogs,' he said.

'Did you ever ride a horse, Grandad?' I asked him.

'Oh, that I did, Pepe. I rode the odd nag, here and there, in the times when horses were used for ploughing. But when I was about your age, I rode to the hunt one Stephen's Day – that's the day after Christmas. You see, one of the locals had the 'flu, and there was a spare mount. I tell you, I jumped at it. That was the first time I tasted hot punch. By God, that was the day.'

We rolled along through the lush Kildare landscape. The Curragh, with its wide, green plains, looked as though it was designed for galloping across. We arrived back to Fordstown full of 'the big plan'. I was very excited, but Grandad was cautious in order to avoid my being disappointed. 'We must think about what to write in your application form,' he said. 'That is the next step.' After that, I would have to prepare for the open day at CHASE. I didn't have much time and I would need plenty of practice.

Grandad borrowed a saddle and a halter from a neigh-bour – I had never used one before, and it would take some getting used to. The Tanseys laughed when they saw me arrive the following afternoon with the battered-looking saddle – they also always rode bareback. But Old

Man Tansey helped me to fit it on to Starlight and every day after that I practised with it, trotting, cantering and galloping around the fields and along the road.

I was nervous on the morning of the open day. I wanted to wear my straw hat with the horses on it, but Grandma said that it might look a bit odd. When we arrived, my name was ticked off a list and I was given a proper jockey's cap with a safety helmet inside it, in case I took a tumble. Grandma, Grandad and I watched as other hopefuls rode around the gallops at Abbeyvale House. When it was my turn, Paddy Deveraux was nearby and gave me a leg up into the saddle.

'She's a trusted mare,' he whispered to me. 'Talk to her with your legs and hands, d'you follow? Give her a "hoosh"; she'll know what to do.' He told me to find a rhythm, and to pick up on the horse's rhythm. I was to take her into a trot, then a canter and finally into a gallop, and then to go for my best time over the five-furlong course. It sounded technical to listen to, but I didn't have to think twice.

I lined up and waited to be given the 'off' by a man holding a stopwatch and a red flag. The flag came down with a swoosh and I leaned forward, staying low in the saddle. It felt great to ride this big, solid horse, as we thundered around the racecourse. It was like being back on El Dorado, riding along the banks of the Putumayo, between the green river and the shade of the tall trees. When we came back around to the starting line, Paddy Deveraux caught the horse's reins and called to the man who held the stopwatch, 'What's the time for Pepe Carroll?'

When he heard my time, he patted the horse, then looked up at me and winked. 'I'll tell you what, lad – you have it in you.'

Chapter 19

I'm making it sound easy, but perhaps we are each made for one thing in life. As Paddy Deveraux would say, 'You've got to be up for it.' And so my story is nearly done, except for the best part.

I had done well enough at the open day to get noticed, so that by the time I was called for an interview with Paddy Deveraux, I knew that it would only be sheer weight of numbers that would keep me from getting a place. And, I had been told, if I didn't get a place the first year I could reapply later.

So when the letter arrived with the blue-and-green CHASE logo on the envelope, I tore it open eagerly. It began, 'Dear Pepe Carroll,' but then I was reminded that my reading still needed to improve. I couldn't understand a word of the rest of it. I dashed into the kitchen and stuck the page in front of Grandma's nose. She took one glance at it, then gasped and ran outside, calling for Grandad. I followed right behind her, nearly stepping on her heels.

'Is it a sick goat?' Grandad came out of the growing tunnel in great haste, his hoe still in one hand.

'The goats will be singing today,' said Grandma. 'Someone wants our little man here for the racetrack.'

'Oh, I can't believe it. Is it possible?' Grandad wanted to see the letter and we went back into the house. There was much crunching and slurping as we all talked and interrupted each other over our lunch of soup, brown bread and goats' cheese salad. I could scarcely believe it! Up until now, we had all been afraid to talk too much about CHASE, in case I wasn't accepted. Now we talked and talked. I could leave the school at Angerstown! My grandparents hadn't realised how much this would mean to me. There was a lot of planning to do. I would need new clothes, and a racing saddle. Of course, it had hardly struck me that I would actually be leaving Fordstown. For eight months, except for short visits some weekends, I would live in the school at CHASE.

I e-mailed Mama and Papa and, by the time I was ready to leave for Abbeyvale House, I got their delighted replies. Papa was working in a bar, and playing occasional gigs, in a place called Saskatoon in Canada. He was fitting his own songs into the act and looking for some company to bring out a CD for him.

He was amazed at my progress and called me *'perito'* in his e-mail, which means 'an expert'. 'You are hardly an expert,' Grandma said to me as we ate our bean stew and potatoes that evening. She didn't want me to get a big head.

'Ah, come on, Mary,' said Grandad, sprinkling sea salt onto his potatoes. 'He has the makings of a champion, with a bit of luck.'

Mama was still working at the hotel, but she was now living in an apartment of her own, with a boyfriend who was English. Mama's e-mail left me worried. Who was this English man? It was strange to know that Mama had a new man, whom I had never met. It seemed that our lives were growing further and further apart.

Now was not the time for worrying, though. I had much to do, and an entire career to plan for.

Chapter 20

There were thirty of us apprentice jockeys at CHASE – eight girls and twenty-two boys. Paddy Deveraux had a son called Liam in the group, and he would become a good friend, but all thirty of us got on well together. It would be a hectic eight months and we were all eager to learn and to work hard. I had a bed, a bedside locker, a desk of my own with a lamp and, best of all, a weekly wage – €60!

While I missed Grandma and Grandad, I wanted to make the grade at CHASE, and that meant working so hard that I collapsed, exhausted, into bed every night. Grandad had given me a present of a mobile phone, so I was able to stay in touch.

Every morning the bell rang at six. We had to get up straight away and give the horses their breakfast before we had our own. I never found it difficult rising early – I was used to early mornings at Fordstown – and the horses were always eager to get out for their morning gallop. This was the most challenging and exciting part of our daily routine, the part of the day that meant the most to me. We got to ride as many as five different horses some days. It was a great pleasure to work with those beautiful horses, and I was never idle. I was all ears and eyes each day, learning and gaining experience. Each day flew by like a fast horse that I could barely catch a glimpse of, gone in a cloud of turf dust.

There were many different areas of 'the industry', as it is called, to learn about – grooming, feeding, exercising and transporting horses, the whole business and financial side of working with horses, as well as medical care and attention. I can never hope to know more than a little about that. I am not a horse doctor, one of those amazing people who can tell what is wrong with an animal simply by looking at its teeth or watching it walking. But we had to learn the basics about blood and urine tests and how to tell if a horse is overheated or distressed. A horse's hooves and legs require special care, so that these powerful and beautiful creatures can perform their magic, galloping from point to point and leaping over fences.

We had to look after ourselves too, especially our diets. It is important for a jockey to stay slim and light, and we had to think of our weight continually. We were expected not to go off into cafés during our time off, indulging ourselves with burgers, chips and sugary drinks. The food policy at the school would have suited my grandparents, with its emphasis on lean meat and fresh vegetables.

We also had regular schooling, of course. I was still way behind in terms of reading and writing, but the other students helped me, particularly with slang words and how to spell the wide variety of curses used about the place! Our teacher, Mrs Byrne, did all she could to help me catch up with the rest of the class. I would have to improve my English drastically in order to read form books and breeding manuals, and to keep up with the *Irish Field* and *Racing Post.* It was not all grind, though. We also had drama, art, swimming and sports classes, so as to give us a break from 'the nags' – the horses.

Not long before the end of the eight months, two of our class left the school – they weren't cut out for 'the life'. But I loved it, and looked forward to the next stage of my apprenticeship. Through the school I met a Mrs Harris of Killantubber Stud. Getting a place with Mrs Harris depended on my graduation, my first race and passing an interview with the Turf Club, the organisation that oversees the racing industry.

The day of my interview was a little scary. Grandad wore his good suit for the occasion and Grandma was also in her best clothes, wearing her hat with a pheasant feather sticking out of it. We had bought my suit in Naas, and Grandad tucked a handkerchief into the top pocket. 'Now you look the part,' he said. He drove us down to the Turf Club office, at the back of the Curragh racecourse. Grandma insisted on spreading clean polythene over the seats of the Landrover, so as not to get our suits dirty.

I waited with Grandad and Grandma outside the

interview room, fidgeting and looking at pictures in a magazine. Then my name was called. 'Good luck, lad,' said Grandad, putting a hand on my shoulder. I went into the interview room, where three stern-looking officials sat behind a long desk.

They asked me all sorts of questions about myself, nodding and giving me a good look over as I spoke. When they asked about Colombia, I did not say anything about AGRA or the commune. I just told them that I used to ride bareback through the jungle. They were pleased that I knew Spanish.

'Do you know, lad,' said one of the officials, 'I some-times hear the roar of the jungle on race days beyond.' He pointed with one of those grand gestures that seem to be a feature of people who love horses. 'That is the whole world to us,' he said. 'And now, if you will leave us to our deliberations, young man?' I nodded and left the room, carefully closing the door behind me.

Grandad and Grandma seemed as nervous as I was as we waited in the hallway. None of us could finish our sentences. This was it. I was either in or out, and I would soon know. When the door opened, the three of us froze. The man who had asked me most of the questions at the interview looked at us seriously, then he reached out and shook my hand. He told me I had the approval of the Turf Club, and congratulated me on gaining a place with Mrs Harris at Killantubber Stud. 'It all depends on your end-of-year exam results,' he said, looking me in the eye. 'Pass your exams and you are in with us. Good luck.'

Grandad and Grandma nearly smothered me when he left, but then they stopped and considered the situation. 'Of course he will pass the exams,' said Grandad.

'Of course,' said Grandma.

'Of course,' I said weakly, echoing their voices.

Chapter 21

Well, to cut a long story short, I did pass the exams, one of only fifteen in the class to get through. The Chairperson of the Licensing Committee made a long speech at our graduation ceremony and presented us with certificates. I went up with Liam Deveraux, Susan Holmes and Johnny Walsh. It was a proud moment for all of us.

Paddy Deveraux shook my hand when the ceremony was over, and punched me softly on the shoulder. 'Pepe, I knew you'd make it. Lad, you're in for an exciting career,' he said brightly. 'He's come a long way,' he added, turning to my grandparents.

He was right too. I *had* come a long way – from my life in the commune in the Colombian jungle to graduating as an apprentice jockey here in Ireland.

It was strange going back to the farm in Fordstown, because this time I knew that I would be going away further from Grandma and Grandad – fifty miles away, to Killantubber. There was an e-mail waiting for me from my papa. He congratulated me on getting through the year at CHASE. Since he had earned some good money recently around Saskatoon, he was coming home for a visit, and he wondered when would be a good time. I replied:

Hello Papa,

¿Gess wat? Got my lisense to ride at last and am finshed with jockey skool CHASE. you cud come over four sekond week septiembre? mis you and lov you all ways,

Pepe.

Grandad went back over it and fixed the spelling, in case Grandma would see it and worry about my progress in English, which was still awful as you can see.

I wrote to Mama also, telling her about my graduation. Then it was time for bed. I had to make my own way to Mrs Harris's stud in Killantubber early the next morning on the country buses. I knew I was lucky to have got a place with Mrs Harris, who had produced quite a few winners from her stables. Divorced from her English husband, she had proved herself the better business operator and was proud of her independence. She seemed very stern, but I had seen her once break into a smile full of warmth. I would have to work hard to prove myself.

The moment I arrived in Killantubber I was put to work. Mrs Harris had bought a horse sired by an Irish stallion – that means its father was Irish. The horse had a Spanish bloodline. When I saw the horse, Golden Boy, I could hardly believe my eyes – it was a beautiful golden colt, just like my old friend El Dorado. It was my job to get her ready for a race, the Apprentice Jockey's Maiden at the Curragh racecourse, in two weeks' time.

I got a bit, reins and a saddle, and took him steadily out of the tackle room, leading with the halter. He had been newly shod and proudly picked his steps with a rhythmic clacking across the cobbled yard. Nothing was hurried; not a spark struck between cobble and horseshoes, as might happen if a horse was rushing or being rushed. Golden Boy, or El Dorado as I would secretly call him, was a beauty. He didn't make shy when I got up on him, and we soon got to know each other as well as El Dorado and I had in Colombia.

I had to keep my mind on the race. I was being thrown in at the deep end, but Mrs Harris, after watching us out practising, entrusted me to give Golden Boy a run.

The two weeks passed quickly. I kept to light meals, watching every little thing I ate, since the last thing I wanted was to be ruled out for being overweight. I had to go for a fitting for my 'colours' – the jockey's racing outfit, including regulation shirt, white trousers and the vital body protector, a padded top with a zip. There was a cravat and a pin for my shirt. I was given Mrs Harris's colours of yellow stars on a green background.

Then, two days before the race, I got a text message from Grandad to say my papa was in Fordstown. I couldn't believe it, but it was true. Mrs Harris said that I could go and visit them, but I decided not to go. Instead I phoned my papa and we talked for an hour. He sounded so positive and said that he couldn't wait to see me after the race. He had written a song for me. There was going to be a party in the pub at Fordstown on race night whether I came first or last.

'I'll sing for you on Saturday, Pepe,' Papa said over the phone.

'Just like when I was small,' I said.

'Do you still remember?' He asked.

'I have never forgotten. How could I? You are my papa and I love you.'

'Oh Pepe, you deserve a better father than me. I've let you down. I haven't been around too much for you, following my dreams instead of making you the centre of my universe.'

'Stop, Papa. You will make me cry,' I said.

Chapter 22

The next morning, like every morning, I was up long before six: bathroom, clothes on, kettle on for a cup of tea for the other lads, then along to the tackroom to get the waterproofs from my locker, and pick up the waterproof sheet for Golden Boy. The morning was still and beautiful, the ground coated in a crisp, sugary frost. Cobwebs hung in the air; the horses breathed white smoke, like dragons in the mist. Behind the trees the orange sun began its slow rise over the eastern horizon.

It was another long day of training and learning. I suddenly became nervous as they loaded Golden Boy into his horsebox in the afternoon for the race the next day. When Dinny Mulligan drove off with him and another colt in the double-horse trailer, I felt the nerves of my stomach creak. Mrs Harris asked me into the dining room for cocoa and oatcakes, but to be honest I could hardly swallow. My throat was dry.

'You'll be fine,' she said confidently. 'Did you talk to your daddy?'

'Yes, Mrs Harris. He is coming to the race tomorrow along with Grandma and Grandad.'

'Of course they are! Okay, Pepe, listen to me. Just take

Golden Boy around any way you like. We don't know much about him yet and I'm not expecting a big finish. Just get him around at his own pace. Give him an outing. That will satisfy me. He's a bit of a gamble but he comes from a good line, and I have a special feeling about him.

'Getting a horse balanced means keeping your balance – every stride and every second has to suit his rhythm. A jockey has got to make a horse want to run for him. You'll keep your eye on things, any little problems? Only you can tell us. I have confidence in you, Pepe. You're well up to it.'

'I will give it my all,' I said, remembering a phrase of Paddy Deveraux' from the school.

I could not sleep that night. I got in and out of bed, checking my kit so many times that the activity ruined my chances of deep sleep. I got an early call to have a quick gallop on whatever was available before breakfast. I had my gallop and then climbed into Mrs Harris's four-wheel drive with the other jockey, Kieran Fahy, and two other lads from the yard. Already people were moving bumper-to-bumper towards the racecourse as we drove through Kilcullen. I felt quite tired. On the drive I kept out of the conversation and managed to doze off, and the sleep really set me up for the day ahead.

It was a pretty good day on the weather front. There were light showers of rain that then eased off, leaving a damp atmosphere about the racecourse. I watched a few races, but could hardly concentrate on them. As the race before mine was announced I went to the changing rooms. Liam Deveraux was there, in a joking mood, as was Susan Holmes, but I had terrible pre-race nerves. Of course, I tried to hide them.

'You look like a ghost.' Paddy Deveraux tapped me on the shoulder. 'Come on, Pepe, this is nothing you haven't done before.'

'I know,' I shrugged, leaning down over my boots and giving them a final rub of a cloth. 'It is the roaring of the crowd that I am worried about.'

'You'll grow to love it,' said Paddy, going over to Liam.

Soon it was my turn to weigh in. This takes place in a special room supervised by the Clerk of the Scales. There is a large, red scales with a huge, clock-like face on it. I sat down on the chair to be weighed, with my saddle in my lap. My weight was five pounds under, so I was given a bigger saddle to bring me up to the average for the race.

My nerves grew worse and worse until I walked out towards the paddock, and suddenly it was as if I had been doing this all my life. Golden Boy, number fifteen – the same as my age – was being walked around inside the railing. I caught a glimpse of Mrs Harris talking to a few other owners and trainers.

There was a big crowd for our event. They were look-ing at the jockeys as well as the horses, since we were newcomers. Golden Boy looked calm and raring to go, and didn't seem bothered by the crowd. I got up on him outside the paddock and settled in, turning a few circles before we moved down towards the starting line. We had done this drill many times.

We lined up in front of the tape. I tightened on the reins, aware of the other runners and riders on either side of me. A few of the jockeys looked nervous, their mounts pawing at the ground, but I began to feel more sure of myself, keeping Golden Boy steady in case he might break the line. I wasn't concerned about the crowd all of a sudden. I had a job to do for Mrs Harris. Everything I had learned at CHASE was coming back to me.

Then a booming voice came over the PA system: 'They are under starting orders for the Apprentice Jockeys' Maiden Race.' I felt awful again, nervous and weak. In a moment I began to sweat and my body was enflamed in heat.

This was it. And I was going to lose it all. I had to calm myself, knowing that Golden Boy would detect my nerves. His ears were up and I had to hold him as he sensed that the other horses were tensing for 'the off'. I said to myself, 'Pepe, forget the Curragh. This is the bank of the Río Putumayo and your old friend El Dorado. Ride as you always have, naturally and with ease. Ride for Mrs Harris, and for Papa, for Grandad and Grandma. Ride for the great Muiscan warrior Pepe Carroll.' As I calmed myself and the horse, the tape suddenly shot up. The race had begun.

We all jolted forward together as I heard the commentary coming over the PA system. Every second counted now. Already my mind was firmly on the finishing line, a wooden post seven furlongs away. We all became very closely packed on the railings. It was a bad situation – no-one wanted to take his mount on the outside, since making a wide arc off the rails would lose you ground.

Liam, on a cranky horse named Captain Haddock, was leading the field. In second position was Susan Holmes on Kerrysilver. There were eleven other runners and riders, all in a huddle, all giving it the utmost. We urged our mounts on with words and with our legs and arms.

The hooves thundered along the ground, but we were packed far too close. I tried to move up with Golden Boy, but he was young and inexperienced like myself. I needed to inspire him. There was so little time – seven furlongs are almost like a long jump at this speed. Every-one was going all out, straining on the bit, poised and keen. Goggles stuck to our faces.

I brought my mind back to the banks of the Putumayo, to El Dorado and me, alone with the river at night. 'Come on, El Dorado,' I yelled. I gave the horse plenty of stirrup to make him want to gallop. 'All out, El Dorado,' I pleaded with him. 'All out.'

We slipped forward one place, then another, and soon I was on the hind flank of Susan's mount, Kerrysilver, who was leading. Then the crowd were up and roaring as we galloped on. I knew that somewhere my papa was watching with Grandma and Grandad. But I had to con-centrate. I must not make any wrong moves. Then the finishing post was ahead of us. Suddenly we shot past it. I had come second.

Susan Holmes had won it on Kerrysilver. They were surrounded by a crowd as we came in. I got a pat on the back from someone as I made my way back behind the bookies. I caught sight of one price for Golden Boy: 7–1. Oh well, I was long odds, but I decided I had won by my own standards – I had had a good run, come in a good place and I had not fallen or caused any other problem for the horse.

Mrs Harris was pleased when I met her, as I dismounted and began unbuckling the bellyband to remove the saddle. One of the stable lads handed me my trench coat and I pulled it on quickly, feeling like a cavalry general. I rubbed down Golden Boy and patted him furiously. Then he was taken away for a wash down since he was out in a foamy sweat. His head was still up and he looked almost startled, as if he wanted to get back in the race.

I picked up the saddle and headed back to the weighing room with it, along with all the other young jockeys, all chatting away excitedly. When I came out I stood silently for a moment to take in what had happened to me. Suddenly everything seemed to disappear – the crowds, the horses – as I saw Papa running towards me.

'Pepe, my son, in second place?' he smiled. 'That horse looked just like your old friend El Dorado.'

'That was me all right,' I grinned proudly, throwing my arms around him.

'I have news. An e-mail from your mother,' he said.

'You read it for me,' I told him.

Dearest Pepe,

Myself and my man, Brian, will be moving to
London in a few months to work in the Russell
Hotel. Yes. I will be close to you. Brian is helping
me to go to university at night and get a degree. I
really have a chance to do this in London. Good
luck with your first race, my little man. And you
may be racing in England? We will be together
more often. More? A lot more.

I love my son always,

Mama xxx

It was the best news I could have got. At last I would see
Mama again!

Chapter 23

On the way to Fordstown Grandma sat in the front with Grandad, while Papa and I sat in the back. At the pub there was hot food. Seán, the barman, winked and said if I ate a big dinner, he would not phone the Curragh and tell the master of the scales! All the men in the pub wanted tips for horses. They said that if I won the Derby or any race at Cheltenham I could drink for free in Fordstown from then on.

The music began and it wasn't long before Papa was called to the microphone with his guitar. He played a few Irish ballads and then said he wanted to sing a song he'd written, 'A Horse Called El Dorado'. I couldn't believe it – it was great, and he belted it out so well that it brought the house down, as they say in that part of County Meath. So much so, in fact, that everyone shouted for an encore, so he sang it again. The chorus goes like this:

Let's all sing with bravado
For a horse called El Dorado
And his rider of renown.
So roll out the barrel,
Each and everyone,
For Pepe Carroll, Pepe Carroll.

Ah, but you should hear it sung.

Papa stayed for two weeks after that great day and night. He went to Dublin a few times to meet some people in the music business and give them copies of his demo CD. I stayed with him in Fordstown. It was a special time. We went to CHASE to see the school, and to Mrs Harris's in Killantubber, and spent a day shopping in Dublin. Then I had to get back to work, and Papa had to return to Canada.

I went with Papa to Busáras, the bus station in Dublin, and we both travelled out on the airport bus. For a long time, he kept his arm on the seat behind me, touching my shoulder and telling me how close he felt to me. He said he would try to do better at his music, to get a band together and move back to Ireland where there might be regular gigs and enough work for him to live.

We checked in his bag, and his guitar in its black case, and went for a bite to eat. I walked to the gate with him when his flight to Canada was called. We had talked so much. Everything was fine between us. Of course, I was sad that he was going.

'It's good about Maria moving to London,' he said, meaning Mama. 'I will try my best to get back to you, little man.'

'Don't worry. I will be okay. I am happy with my work, just like you.'

'Ah, you're too good to me, Pepe. Too good,' he said, becoming sad. 'I seem to be always just getting talking to you when I'm about to leave you. Isn't it awful? Your old papa is an awful restless wanderer. Didn't I sing "I was Born Under a Wandering Star" at the big night for you in Fordstown?'

'That is the way you are,' I said.

'Listen to me, I will be back again soon.' He hugged me. 'Let's be men and save our tears for when we meet again.'

'Okay,' I said, about to overflow. 'Take care of yourself, Papa. For me.'

'I will. And you take care of yourself for me. Send me an e-mail real soon.'

Then Papa got up and walked through the barrier. I watched as he turned around for the last time. 'Hey, I forgot to ask, Pepe. Was my song any good?'

'Your song "A Horse Called El Dorado"?' I asked timidly.

'Yes,' he answered.

'It was the business, Papa. It was the business.'

'Ride a winner for me, okay?' He smiled. He turned to give me a wave. I felt he might make it back to Ireland, and somehow I would have my parents close by again, just like when I was so young in Colombia. I felt a sting of loneliness, but I had grown up a lot over the last few years. Secretly I felt proud. I just wanted to get back to Golden Boy, my El Dorado, and the stable. I love my work. I love being a lad in a yard. Maybe some day I *will* ride a winner in a big race.

MORE BOOKS FROM
THE O'BRIEN PRESS

From MARITA CONLON-MCKENNA

Winner: **Bisto Book of the Year Award**

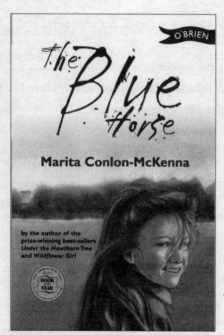

Katie Connors is a traveller. All her life her family has moved around from one site to the next. Life is hard on the road but it's the life they love and know best. Then one night the family's caravan burns down and they are left destitute. Katie must fit into a new, settled life in a house. But will she be accepted?

From MORGAN LLYWELYN

When Ger Casey sneaks into the Dublin Horse Show and sees Star Dancer at dressage practice, he is fascinated. Somehow, some day *he* is going to ride like that! Suzanne O'Gorman, the rider of Star Dancer, has a dream too – to ride in the Olympics. They both have difficulties to overcome – Ger's family, friends and background, Suzanne's sudden strange fear of jumping. Brought together by their love of horses, the two are determined to succeed, no matter what!

'Will appeal to all budding riders as well as lovers of a good story'
BELFAST TELEGRAPH